100 DARK HORROR STORIES
JONAH BUCK

Special thanks to Brittani

Cover Design by James, GoOnWrite.com

This is a work of fiction. Names, characters, businesses, places, events, locales, and incidents are either the products of the author's imagination or used in a fictitious manner. Any resemblance to actual persons, living or dead, or actual events is purely coincidental.

100 Dark Horror Stories by Jonah Buck

www.jonahbuck.com

Contents

DONATED TO SCIENCE

SANDY BEACHES

QUANTITY HAS A QUALITY ALL ITS OWN

COVERED WAGONS

EARWORM

LIGHTS OUT

BOB LARSON: PARANORMAL INVESTIGATOR

HEIST

RISE AGAIN

YOU NEVER CAN TELL

TAR PITS

SURVIVORS

RING

SWAT

UPON NIGHT'S LEATHERY WINGS

USS ARMSTRONG

PRONUNCIATION

MIRROR, MIRROR

GONE FISHING

CAVIAR

FOG

REWARD

XIII

UPSTREAM

FLINT

CUTTHROAT COMPETITION

IDOL HANDS

MAKEUP

DRAGON SLAYER

BLACK PICKUP TRUCK

DENTISTRY

KILL THE BEAST

LOVE LETTERS

SHOW AND TELL

SPECIAL FORCES

WHAT IS IT, GIRL?

ZZZZZZZZZZZZZZZZZ

SUMMONING RITUAL

PROTECTOR

SCARECROWS

MOVING TRUCK

POWDER

CHOP CHOP

A WORD FROM OUR SPONSORS

CERTAIN LINEAGES

MOTE

JEWELRY

ROMAN BATHS

UNDEAD

THE ISLAND GOD

SHOPPING SPREE

SOME PIG

TRACKER

TOXIC

WRONG TURN AT HOG MOUNTAIN

CAPTAIN SAMARITAN

MOLOC

WEARY

SPECIAL EFFECTS

LANDSCAPE

MAROONED

PRINCESS HONEYSMOOCH AND THE FAIRY KINGDOM

ONLINE DATING

VERMIN

THREE WEIRD SISTERS

ANNIVERSARY

HUNTING THE SHAPESHIFTER

LOOK WHAT THE CAT DRAGGED IN

SPELUNKING

IMAGINARY FRIENDS FOR SALE

LIVE UPDATE

WAITING ROOM

ANYTHING AT ALL, SWEETHEART

GEORGE

<u>ONE</u>
GENTLY USED

I stood in the middle of the lot, near a giant, inflatable gorilla. I must have been gawping at the merchandise because a salesman sidled up to me.

The kid looked like he'd just graduated, and his face was fighting a war of attrition with acne. The acne was winning.

"It's time for Big Mike's annual April sale. We're overflowing with deals on selected inventory. Be sure to check out our Dealer's Choice item. We'd have to be crazy to have such low prices," he rattled off a spiel that he'd no doubt memorized from a notecard.

"Give me the skinny on the Dealer's Choice." We started walking to another section of the lot.

"The Dealer's Choice is a Model DT-10, with a sleek, metallic finish and upholstered interior. The previous owner was Big Mike's very own grandmother. Last used on a drive to the church, this luxurious DT-10 has minimal wear and tear. It's a steal at any price."

"Little old lady only used it once. Never heard that before." What turnip truck did he think I just fell off of?

The salesman was unfazed. He had a pitch to get through. If he lost his place now, he might have to start over.

"Perfect for you, your spouse, or up to three children, the roomy interior is stylish and comfortable. Big Mike guarantees you'll love the mahogany accents. The exterior's sleek, timeless lines make the Model DT-10 a classic, and the scratch-resistant finish ensures that your purchase will remain in perfect condition. The Model DT-10 can handle any terrain, from mud to rocks."

"What're your pricing options?"

"With our Dealer's Choice item, we'll take no money down and no interest for twelve months."

"Mind opening it up? I wanna check the interior."

The salesman produced a key, and the door popped open. I took a good, long gander.

"There's some scratch marks on the interior upholstery. That knock the price down any further?"

"Interested in buying? We should go to my office."

I started to follow him past the Big Mike's Gently Used Coffins sign toward the showroom.

TWO
SPRING FEVER

Ms. Franklin sneezed. It was not a polite sneeze. It was loud and it was messy and it nearly doubled her over. A few kids on the playground stopped their joyful screaming and running just long enough see whether or not Ms. Franklin had exploded or not. Then, they went back to shrieking like howler monkeys.

"Bless you," one of the other third grade teachers said.

As if on cue, Ms. Franklin sneezed again, even harder this time.

"You all right?" The other teacher looked at her with obvious concern. A cold could spread through an elementary school like radioactive space Ebola. If one person was sick, it usually meant everyone else on the staff would have it within the week.

"I'm fine," Ms. Franklin said, holding a hand up before straightening herself. "It's just these damn spring allergies. Spring fever or something."

In truth, Ms. Franklin didn't look fine. Her skin was pale, and her hair was wet and limp around her face, plastered in place with sweat. And her eyes were red, shockingly red. She dabbed at her nose with a wadded-up tissue.

"My kids and I were going to do an art project after recess. Do you want to send a group over to me until you recover? You're looking a little green around the gills."

Ms. Franklin let loose another room clearer of a sneeze before answering. "Thanks, but no thanks. I've got my kids doing a special reading project that they need to work on. I might have bitten off more than I can chew this time. There's an interactive portion and everything. Gonna have them act out some scenes. It'll be fun, but the time...*poof*."

"I hear that."

"Speaking of which, I might pull them in from recess a little early." Ms. Franklin blew her whistle hard enough to hurt everyone's ears and readied her command and conquer voice. "Okay kids, let's head inside."

There was a chorus of groans as games ended prematurely and friends said quick goodbyes.

"What sort of project are you working on? I thought you were busy trying to get everyone prepared for state testing."

"Something historical. Just for fun."

One of the girls came up to them. "Ms. Franklin, I drew you a picture!" The crayon drawing featured a bunny rabbit with sparkly goo-goo eyes.

Ms. Franklin sneezed again. Despite covering her mouth, a fine mist of snot and spit landed on the drawing.

"Sorry, Lindsey," Ms. Franklin said. "Ready to work on your report about the Inquisition?"

The little girl nodded as Ms. Franklin led everyone back indoors.

Inside Ms. Franklin, the demon possessing her body sniffled. This assignment was a bunch of crap. The Boss knew he was allergic to happiness and kindness, and the school was filthy with the stuff. It would take at least until summer to finish corrupting these children.

Ms. Franklin sneezed again as one of her students held the door open.

THREE
WITCH TRIALS

"And so, for your crimes against man and God alike, you are hereby sentenced to death," the colonial magistrate said from his perch atop the gallows. "Do you have any final words, witch?"

"Please, you have to listen to me. I am not a witch. I swear it. I swear it upon the Good Book and upon my very soul. Please, don't do this," Mary Hollings said through the black sack covering her head.

"It's time," the magistrate said. The executioner pulled the lever, and Mary Hollings plunged through the trap door. There was a snap that echoed through the whole of Salem.

Jane Eastman looked away so she wouldn't have to see Mary's feet twitch a foot above the ground any more. It could have been her just as easily. She was lucky the finger of accusation hadn't been pointed at her, or she and Mary might have switched places. Frankly, she was ashamed to be standing among the crowd. But to avoid the spectacle would only serve to draw suspicion upon herself.

The truth was, Jane had dabbled in the occult and the forbidden. She'd also been known to question some of the teachings of the church, though never too loudly. By itself, with nothing else, that was enough to hang people these days.

But was Jane a witch? No. Not really. She had an interest in the arcane and she liked to speak her mind, but she wasn't one to go prancing nude under the light of the full moon. She didn't commune with the devils of hell around a bubbling cauldron.

Standing on the gallows, the colonial magistrate watched as Mary's feet stopped their spasmodic, floating dance. Urine dribble down her leg and stained her shoes. Someone near the front of the crowd snickered at that.

Animals, the lot of them.

These were dangerous times for someone like Jane, and she knew it. She thought she could see the light at the end of the tunnel. But it would only take a spark to reignite that fire and begin the frenzy anew all over again.

She had to stay with the crowd. She had to keep her head down. She couldn't dissent too loudly, or it would almost certainly be her up on the gallows next. It was a simple matter of saying the right things and avoiding suspicion.

The magistrate cleared his throat and addressed the crowd. "Ladies and gentlemen of Salem, it has been a pleasure working with you once more. However, while I have all of you gathered, I want to make sure that we all agree on the same story. It's very simple. There was a witch scare, and we were overzealous. Mistakes were made, and we now see the errors of our ways. False accusations led to hysteria and lapses in the normal judicial process. We're all very sorry and feel properly chastised. Understood?"

The crowd nodded.

"Good," the magistrate said. "With the last of the non-witches dead, the town is finally ours. But I urge you to remain cautious. There may yet be those among us who would foil our plans. Stick to the story, but remain vigilant."

Jane swallowed hard. Even if it was just for show, their story had worked. The witches had full control now.

FOUR

NOT TRAINED FOR THIS

Lieutenant Nichols stood in front of his remaining men. He was their commanding officer now, since Major Pemberton was missing and presumed dead. The unit had started out with over fifty men. Now, they were down to less than twenty.

They weren't trained for this. No one was trained for this. They didn't know what to expect when they were deployed to this godawful place, but Nichols never envisioned the slow, gruesome slide toward oblivion that they'd experienced so far.

If they didn't kill the creature soon, it would end them all. The problem was, the thing was massive. Their weapons couldn't do a thing against it. Every time they encountered the hulking beast, it seized at least one more man, carrying him off to face an awful fate.

Nichols eyed the remaining soldiers. They were a beaten down, sorry looking lot. They'd seen their friends and comrades killed in some of the nastiest ways imaginable. Nichols himself had seen Private Chung eaten before his very eyes, swallowed whole by the monster that ruled these lands. Others had been melted down to hot grease, as if struck by a blast of flame from one of the dragons of old.

"I have a plan," Nichols said.

"*Man*," Simmons said, drawing the word out, long and skeptical. They were on the verge of breaking, if not mutiny. A few more days of this, and it would be every man for himself. The unit couldn't continue to take losses like this.

"Stow it, Private," Nichols said, summoning every ounce of authority he had left. The grumbling from the men quieted.

"What do you have for us, LT?" Winslow asked.

Thank God for Winslow. He'd been through hell on this deployment just like everyone else, but he'd somehow found a little corner of zen. Maybe he'd simply come to accept his likely fate.

"Our guns won't kill this thing, but I think we can bring it down another way We use the local infrastructure. The parts we can access anyway. It'll take coordination between multiple teams, but we need to lure it to a particular sector, rupture one of the water lines, and then hit it with some of the juice out of the electrical grid while it's wet. We can fry it."

The men didn't look hopeful exactly, but some of the fearful discontent started to fall away as they considered the option.

Suddenly, the earth rumbled and everyone went very still.

***

Mallory Browne opened the door to her son's bedroom and glanced around. Her eyes fell on the little green army men arrayed on the floor. They were assembled like they were all listening to a little leader. Her eyes looked elsewhere.

For a moment, she thought she'd heard voices in here. Maybe the neighbors just had their television on too loud. Maybe she was just losing her mind. She'd been stressed since Ryan's trip to the doctor. After his father told him to stop melting army men on the grill, Ryan had swallowed a couple of them while pretending to be a dinosaur. She really ought to just get rid of the things. She looked around one more time and shut the door.

Nichols breathed a sigh of relief. Then, he pointed at Winslow.

"Corporal, take a few men and start stripping some of the wiring. We can kill this thing yet."

FIVE

BARFLIES

Vernon walked down the stinking, dark alley. Dusk had finally settled in over the city, and the streetlights had blazed to life. Not in the alley, though. The alley remained a brickwork cave of darkness, a haven for feral cats. It smelled of warm dumpster trash and old hobo urine. Vernon knew from experience that a good rain wouldn't wash the odors away; it only made them wet and soggy.

About halfway down the alley was a metal door embedded in the brickwork. Vernon stopped in front of the door and knocked. A slat opened in the door and a pair of red-rimmed eyes stared out at Vernon.

"Who is it?" The voice came from behind the thick door.

"I'm with the Prohibition Bureau," Vernon said.

The door opened. "That joke wasn't funny the first hundred times, either," Felix the doorman said.

Vernon walked into the underground bar. The place didn't have any sort of license. Its continued existence relied mostly on the fact the cops and city officials didn't want to trek through the crummy, rundown maze of alleyways and old tenements to get here.

It was Vernon's favorite place to grab a drink, though. The bar was always quiet, and it was open 'til dawn.

There were a couple other customers sitting at the bar. Vernon pulled up a seat a respectful distance away. Nobody was here to make friends. He gave a curt nod to his companions. One of them returned the nod. The other was too deep into his drink to even look at the new arrival.

The barman sidled up to the counter. He didn't say anything. He never did.

"I'll take a cold one," Vernon said. The barman disappeared into the back cooler.

Vernon didn't ask for a brand name. It wasn't that kind of place. He'd take whatever he got, and he'd like it. If he complained, Felix would drag his butt outside and shut the door. It was nice here, though. No forced pleasantries. No televisions blasting out sports commentary. No crappy Americana nailed to the walls in an attempt at décor. The bar didn't even have a formal name. It was dedicated to one thing and one thing only, slaking thirst.

Vernon slapped some crumpled bills on the table as the barman hauled his drink in from the back. The barman collected the money and handed a few crusty-looking coins back. Then, he hoisted the sedated body over to Vernon.

Vernon pushed the young woman's hair away from her neck, and he barred his fangs. Time to settle in for another long night with the other barflies.

<u>SIX</u>

CNIDARIANS

Veronica Kwan stared out the vessel's window into the pitch blackness beyond. In the distance, she could see occasional flashes and pulses, bioluminescent creatures in the stygian gloom. It was impossible to gauge distance out there in the darkness. The creatures flashing warnings and mating signals could have been close and tiny or distant and massive.

Treated oxygen pumped out of the filters, harsh and processed. The compressed air was keeping the science vessel's crew alive, but it wasn't particularly pleasant. Each breath was stale and slightly oily somehow.

Veronica specialized in deep sea biology. Specifically, she studied cnidarians, jellyfish. Jellyfish were truly remarkable creatures in part because of their enduring simplicity. They showed up in the fossil record some six hundred million years ago. Over half a billion years ago. Before dinosaurs were a glimmer in the planet's eye, jellyfish were swimming and pulsing through the primordial seas.

Today, they were found all over the world, teeming through every section of the sea. That was despite the fact that they had no brain. No eyes. No real organs to speak of. Just a hungry little bag, floating through the ocean. The fact that they regularly ate fish and crustaceans, animals that were technically much more advanced than themselves, seemed to spit in the face of evolution. The simple, venerable jellyfish was little more than a mouth, and that was all it needed.

Veronica had jumped at the chance to go on this mission. It was a little out of her bailiwick, but it was an incredibly exciting offer. She could go further, deeper than anyone else in her field had ever gone before, potentially witnessing aspects of nature never seen by human eyes.

That was the pitch the space administration made. They wanted someone who understood simple creatures that could live and thrive in the blackest, emptiest void of space, and they thought

11

an expert in cnidarians would be their best bet. The creatures of the void, if they were like anything on earth, would probably be closest to those roving, insatiable mouths deep in the sea.

Veronica looked out the window as the red emergency lights flashed. The life support systems were beginning to fail as the massive space creature's digestive enzymes ate through the hull, bit by bit. The ship hadn't been able to escape after becoming ensnared in those beautiful, glowing tentacles, and there was no chance now that they were caught in the beast's gullet.

She focused on the view outside, visible through the giant space jellyfish's transparent skin. She focused on the beauty of the flashing lights and spectral pulses. There was nothing she or anyone else on the crew could do now. It was best to focus on something other than their impending digestion.

SEVEN

CURED

Dr. Gregor Nielson clapped along with everyone else as Dr. Eva Kartik walked up the podium stairs to receive her award. There were at least nominally other contenders for the prize, but everyone knew Dr. Kartik would win.

Gregor was one of those contenders, and he didn't begrudge Dr. Kartik one bit. His work on skin grafts and cosmetic reconstruction was important. He'd received many accolades in the last few months. But Dr. Kartik led the team the cured the zombie plague.

Some billion people had succumbed to the virus, rising again as the "living dead." It was a complete misnomer, scientifically speaking. The victims weren't technically dead, but the ghastly term had been used since the very beginning of the outbreak, and it stuck. Even members of the scientific community used the phrase sometimes.

Another two billion people had perished in circumstances related to the virus. Eaten alive, mostly. But lack of food, destroyed infrastructure, and mass rioting had taken their toll as well. Most of the world had fallen into a state of anarchy or martial law. Only Dr. Kartik's cure had saved the rest of humanity.

Looking around, Gregor saw a number of people who had benefitted from his own research after the plague. The so-called zombies almost always sustained grievous injuries while afflicted with the disease. Bites. Gun shots. Burns. The list went on. His reconstructive techniques and skin grafting formula allowed most people to recover some semblance of their former appearance. Thousands of surgeons were using methods he pioneered. It was an important step for many people to return their lives to normality.

But he would be the first to admit that the Dr. Kartik's vaccine was of far greater importance. Gregor himself had benefited from it. He could remember very early on in the outbreak, when no one knew what they were dealing with yet. A breach in his hazmat suit. The seemingly dead man's teeth buried in his arm. The fever.

Everything after that was just a red mist, with individual flashes of memory, like scattered snapshots. His own work would have been impossible if the soldiers hadn't found him in the shattered remains of the government biohazard shelter and injected him with the cure.

Dr. Kartik began her speech after the applause finally died down. Gregor only listened to it with half an ear, though. This awards ceremony was proof that the methods he'd developed were well understood. His work was done.

Back in his hotel room, he had a small container of phosgene tablets. The poison would produce a relatively painless death, especially in conjunction with the sedatives he'd acquired.

Dr. Kartik had cured him of the disease. The virus was no longer in his body. But he still had those scattershot memories. He could remember before he was bitten insisting his family stay in the biohazard shelter because it was the safest place. And then, after the bite, there was a brief parting of the red curtain in his mind. One of the clearest memories he possessed. Gregor would never forget eating his family, never forget the way they tasted.

He was cured. Thanks to his own research, he was even relatively whole. But some afflictions had no cure.

EIGHT

EGYPTIAN ARTIFACTS

The whole museum was in an uproar. Someone had stolen one of the mummies from the Egyptology exhibit. Queen Ahmose and her sarcophagus were both gone.

As the lead curator of the exhibit, Dr. Stanley Phips now found himself in considerable hot water. The police had been in to question him several times already this morning.

He didn't think he was a suspect; he simply knew the exhibit backwards and forwards, including its security systems. The museum director had been in and out of his office too, sometimes quiet and melancholy and sometimes railing against whoever was responsible.

It was definitely a blow to the museum's reputation. There were already stories in the press describing the situation. A news van was parked out front near the police vehicles. A couple of donors had already called to express their concern, and another museum had called to ask if the artifacts they had on loan could be returned any sooner.

That wasn't why Stanley was sweating at his desk, though. He was the man who'd discovered Ahmose's tomb. He was the one who opened it and first found her lying in state, exquisitely preserved. He was the one who read the hieroglyphics carved on the walls. He was the sole survivor from that expedition. This matter wasn't so simple as just a heist.

There was a compounding factor, though. He'd found a note on his desk this morning, before anyone realized Queen Ahmose was gone. He didn't dare check it again, not with the police coming in and out of his door. He already had it memorized, anyway.

Midnight. Tell no one. Come alone. Then, it gave an address.

He glanced at the clock. Then, he looked outside. The sun was beginning to set. He knew he would go. He had to go. After that night in the tomb, he knew what was at stake. So many things could go wrong.

A few hours later, he arrived at the address on the note. It was an old furniture factory on the edge of the city, abandoned years ago. The lock on the gate had been snapped off. He eased inside. He had a few items in his coat pockets, items he thought he would need. He might never get another shot at this.

He slipped inside the dark structure. There were no lights. The sound of his feet echoed down the dusty hallways. Then, he saw it.

Ahmose's coffin lay on an old assembly line in the heart of the abandoned building. He took another step closer when a hand with the texture of beef jerky landed on his shoulder. Stanley whipped around and yanked the items out of his pocket.

"Darling," Ahmose whispered, her sepulchral voice as raspy as the desert wind.

"My love," he said, handing her the small bouquet and chocolates.

He'd originally thought that bringing her back to the museum would be the best way to see her. But he'd been wrong; he needed to steal her away from there before the other curators discovered their forbidden love. Stanley had been forced to kill all the other members of the original expedition after they saw the two of them together in the tomb. Now that she was free at last, they could truly be together.

NINE

IT EATS

Andrew walked down the hotel hallway. The cheap, oddly patterned carpet swallowed up the sound of his footsteps. He was pretty sure that the hotel's owners had chosen the garish carpet because it would help disguise stains rather than on any sort of interior decorating merits.

A couple of the doors on either side of the hallway had DO NOT DISTURB signs dangling from their handles. Most didn't. There weren't many people staying at this dump. Andrew could hear muffled laugh tracks and droning news anchors behind some of the doors, signs that the other visitors were enjoying the free cable the hotel's signs advertised.

Andrew was too restless to sit and vegetate in front of the idiot box, though. He should be trying to get some shut eye, but it just wasn't happening on the hotel's lumpy, squishy mattress. The deal was going down tomorrow, and it would make him or break him. The crate full of guns sitting in the back of his van would give him an in with the organization. Or the broker would shoot him in the face and dump his body in the aqueduct before taking everything. Being the bagman was not a fun assignment.

What he needed was something to drink. He wandered down the hallway in the direction of the front office. He remembered seeing a vending machine not too far from the stairwell, right next to an ice maker. He wanted something harder than a cold soda, but it was a bad idea to go cruising around in that van too much. A simple traffic stop could ruin everything.

A moment later, he found the vending machine. The humming obelisk offered ice cold cola, sports drinks, and water. Andrew dug his wallet out and found a creased dollar bill and some change. He'd get a sports drink. They all tasted like goat spit, but they didn't have any caffeine that would keep him up even later.

He fed the change into the machine's slot, and then he straightened the dollar out and pushed it into the feeder. The vending machine whirred, and Andrew's dollar disappeared. He punched the button for the red-flavored drink.

The machine whirred again, and there was a *KER-CHUNK* from somewhere inside. Andrew bent down to take his drink from the slot, but nothing happened. No drink appeared.

Son of a bitch.

Andrew stabbed the money return button. Nothing happened. He pushed the drink button again. Nothing happened. He placed his hands on the side of the machine and rattled it. Nothing happened.

He'd heard something fall free inside the machine. Maybe it just got stuck. He didn't have another dollar, and even if he did, he wasn't about to waste it by feeding that one to the vending machine, too.

Getting down on his knees, Andrew stuck his hand into the drink slot. His fingers felt around, probing upward, searching for his drink. He adjusted himself and managed to get his arm up into the machine to about his elbow. Then, he felt something.

It was warm and moist. Its texture was like the Andrew's grandmother's hands, wrinkled and veiny and thin as cheap fast food napkins.

Then, Andrew heard a crunch. He yelped as his arm was yanked further into the slot. His hand suddenly felt warm and slick, like it had been covered in hot syrup, and an astonishing pain followed. Andrew cursed and tried to pull his arm back.

He got a couple of inches back, but then it was sucked further inside. It felt like a giant mouth was sucking his arm like a lollipop. A mouth full of teeth. Andrew jerked forward again, braining himself against the front of the vending machine. The light behind the sign flickered for a second and then came back.

Andrew managed to scream exactly once before his head smashed into the front of the machine again, knocking him unconscious. The vending machine continued to spool his arm inward, crunching bone and snapping tendons where necessary. It paused for a moment when it reached his shoulder, but with enough pulling and tugging from inside, it managed to continue, whirring the whole time.

When it was done, the garish carpet hid the stains remarkably well.

TEN

PAPA BEAR'S NEW SHIRT

One morning, Papa Bear woke up in his cave and started to get dressed for a big day in the woods. But then he realized that he couldn't find his new shirt.

"Hmmm," said Papa Bear. "Where did I leave my new shirt?"

He walked across the cave and asked Mama Bear. "Good morning. Have you seen my new shirt, Mama Bear?"

Mama Bear thought for a moment. "No, I have not seen your new shirt. What color is it?"

"It is red," Papa Bear said.

"Maybe Baby Bear has seen your new shirt," Mama Bear said.

Papa Bear nodded and walked to the cave's entrance, where Baby Bear was playing. "Good morning. Have you seen my new shirt, Baby Bear?" Papa Bear asked.

Baby Bear thought for a moment. "No, I have not seen your new shirt. Does your shirt have a pattern?"

"My new shirt is flannel," Papa Bear said.

"Maybe Mr. Rabbit has seen your new shirt," Baby Bear said.

Papa Bear nodded and walked outside the cave. He found Mr. Rabbit standing near his burrow. "Good morning. Have you seen my new shirt, Mr. Rabbit?"

Mr. Rabbit thought for a moment. "No, I have not seen your new shirt. What size is it?"

"It is very big because I am very big," Papa Bear said.

"Maybe Ms. Frog has seen your shirt," Mr. Rabbit said.

Papa Bear nodded and walked to the pond. He found Ms. Frog sitting by the side of the water. "Good morning. Have you seen my new shirt, Ms. Frog?"

Ms. Frog thought for a moment. "No, I have not seen your new shirt. Where did you leave it last?"

Now Papa Bear thought for a moment. "I think I know where I left my new shirt now. Thank you for helping me remember, Ms. Frog."

"You're welcome," Ms. Frog said.

Papa Bear walked away from the pond and started through the woods. He found the old campsite and looked in the torn tent. There was his new shirt. It was still on the mauled corpse inside. The dead man's gnawed face was a featureless chasm of crimson gore, chewed away and scored with trenched rows where Papa Bear's fangs scraped against the corpse's skull. Flies exploded out of the tent in a vile, black cloud. The man's rotting skin tried to slough off like wet bacon, leaving behind stinking grease and maggot-chewed gristle.

"Here is my new shirt," Papa Bear said, pulling it off the camper. He put it on, ready to start a big, new day at last.

ELEVEN

FIXER UPPER

"Oh, I think we can work with this," Saul said, rubbing his hands together. "We can flip this in no time."

"It'll take some work," Julia said. She eyed the dilapidated home. The FOR SALE sign leaned crookedly in the overgrown front yard. An addendum had been added. SOLD.

Ivy had grown over a significant portion of the front side of the house. One window was busted out, and the ivy was starting to poke its way inside.

Once upon a time, the place had been a grand Southern home. Maybe not a mansion exactly, but large and comfortable. A wide porch, now sagging and partly rotted, greeted them like the maw of a great beast.

Julia moved up the walkway toward the entrance. This place was a strong breeze from falling over. But Saul was right. They could make this work. She'd seen worse, and they'd found ways to flip those, too. This was what they did.

Saul scooted around her and picked his way up the porch. Despite appearances, it didn't immediately collapse. He made his way through the front entrance and disappeared.

Julia continued to look around the weeds outside for a few more minutes. She was about to investigate an old stone well in the front yard when she heard a ghastly moan from inside the house.

"OOOooooOOooOOOOooh."

Julia sighed and made her way to the house's entryway. "You do this every time," she said.

"OOoooOOOOOOooch," Saul said again.

She feigned like she was going to punch him on the arm, and he flinched away. "We need to finish evaluating everything."

"Check this out," Saul said, disappearing around a corner. Julia gave a much more dramatic sigh and followed him.

There was a hatchet embedded in the wall near the kitchen. The head was rusted and dark, and it looked like it would be halfway impossible to pry it out.

"Lovely," Julia said.

"Pretty great, right?" Saul asked, gesturing.

"We can make this work," Julia said. She heard a vehicle pull up outside, and she went to the broken window. The home's new owners had just pulled up.

Saul floated through the wall to see what she was looking at. "A few arcane symbols written in blood. A few bones buried along the right ley lines. We'll have this place flipped over to fully haunted in no time. These fixer upper yuppies will never know what hit them."

"Let's gct to work," Julia said, fading away into the shadows. They'd have this house flipped to the powers of the netherworld in no time.

TWELVE

AMAZING ARACHNOID ISSUE #47

Finnegan crept through the museum's second floor, using his flashlight only when he needed it. The security system was down; he'd seen to that, but there might still be a guard or two. He rounded a corner and nearly crashed straight into Li.

"Cripes," Finnegan said, his heart racing. "What are you doing here? You're supposed to take care of the guards."

"I already did," Li said. "They're tied up in the break room. Somebody will find them in the morning."

"Good. Help me get some of these paintings off the wall. We need to get everything we can back to the truck in the next couple of hours."

"I'm thinking we should just leave," Li said.

"Why the hell would you say that?" Stan asked. "You said you took care of the guards. I turned off all the cameras and alarms. There's nothing to worry about. Just start grabbing art."

"I just have a bad feeling about this," Li said.

"Everything's taken care of. Just move."

"But what about…the Amazing Arachnoid?"

Finnegan snorted. "Nothing to it. Some scientist gets bitten by a radioactive spider, gets superpowers, and starts fighting crime? Bunch of crap. It's a myth. An urban legend. Now will you get going?"

Li nodded, but he didn't look convinced. He moved into a different room, and Finnegan heard the sounds of picture frames being pried off the wall.

Perfect. He started his own work, setting his flashlight down and pulling out a crowbar. The artworks were secured to the wall with heavy bolts, and he had to lever them off one at a time.

He was about halfway through pulling the first painting off the wall when he realized that he couldn't hear Li working anymore. Finnegan stopped his own efforts and listened. He cursed under his breath and put the crowbar down.

Walking into the next room, he looked around for his partner. Li was nowhere to be seen. Finnegan went back and grabbed his flashlight again. He was loath to turn it on and draw attention to his presence, but he didn't see what choice he had.

He snapped the light on and shone it around. Li was gone.

"What the hell?" Finnegan muttered to himself.

Suddenly, he heard something. Not in the next room. Not behind him. Above him. He whipped the flashlight up and saw Li's mummified body attached to the ceiling, glued there with some sort of sticky substance. All the liquid had been drained out of the man's body, leaving a leathery husk of skin and bones. The sound Finnegan heard was the dried tendons on Li's body creaking against each other.

Finnegan ran. He didn't wait to gather his tools. He didn't slow down to grab the painting he'd loosened. He didn't try to pull Li's body down. He just ran.

But he slammed into something in the doorway. He came to a violent stop. Finnegan tried to bounce off and keep going, but he was stuck. His skin and clothes gripped the strands of silk. Thrashing and shouting, giving up on any pretense of stealth, Finnegan tried to free himself.

A figure unfolded itself from the shadows and skittered toward Finnegan. The light from the flashlight lying on the floor revealed skewed features. Multiple eyes erupted from the man's skull. Pedipalps and chelicera hung from his cavernous mouth.

Finnegan screamed as the Amazing Arachnoid saved the day again.

THIRTEEN
PAULINE

"Pretty girl," Sarah said. "Can you say 'pretty girl' for me, Pauline?"

Pauline didn't say anything. She paced around on the perch in her bird cage, watching Sarah. Mostly she just had her eyes on the treat in Sarah's hand.

"Can you say, 'Pauline wants a treat' for your mama?" Sarah asked.

She didn't really expect a response from Pauline. Only a few bird species tried to mimic people, and Pauline wasn't one of them. Still, Pauline liked the attention. If she was feeling gregarious, she'd let Sarah stroke her head while her cage was being cleaned.

Sarah held the treat out, and Pauline took it out of the palm of her hand. Keeping her arm held out, Sarah let Pauline step onto her wrist and shimmy her way up Sarah's arm until she was out of the cage.

Stepping over to the window, Sarah put Pauline down on another perch next to a food bowl. That would keep Pauline happy for a while. A man in jeans and a dark sweatshirt walked past on the sidewalk, headphones stuffed in his ears. Sarah adjusted the curtains a bit so Pauline could see outside better.

In truth, Sarah shouldn't have kept Pauline. She'd been on a hike one day and she found a wild baby bird with a broken wing at the bottom of a tree. The little fledgling barely had its downy feathers, and it was making pathetic screeching sounds. Sarah knew the poor thing wouldn't survive long on its own like that, so she bundled it up and took it home to nurse it back to health.

Pauline mostly made a full recovery. Her wing didn't mend properly, so she couldn't fly, but she wasn't in any serious pain. Even if she could take to the sky, Sarah couldn't release her. Pauline was basically domesticated. She never learned how to survive in the wild from other birds. Left to her own devices, she'd starve.

So, Sarah kept her. Pauline wasn't a pet exactly. She still had too much of the wild in her. But she trusted Sarah, and they were friends after a fashion. At this point, Sarah wouldn't want to give Pauline up. It was a lot of work to keep a big, semi-wild bird happy and fed, but it was worth it in the end. Sarah had grown as attached to Pauline as a mother hen to her chicks.

She started laying down fresh newspaper at the bottom of Pauline's cage when a headline caught her eye. *POLICE SEARCH FOR CANNIBAL MURDERER. Local authorities continue to seek information regarding prolific serial killer known for cutting off portions of victims' bodies. It is believed the amputated sections are eventually eaten, based on disturbing, knife-marked bones recently discovered.*

Sarah tsked to herself. "Can you believe what the world's coming to, Pauline?"

Pauline didn't answer. She just kept staring out the window with her keen bird eyes.

"It took the police *months* to find those bones. Lazy good-for-nothings."

Sarah went to the fridge and pulled a slab of human thigh out. She sliced a nice meaty section off and put it in Pauline's bowl.

The vulture gobbled it down while Sarah stroked her bald, featherless head.

FOURTEEN
SKYSCRAPER

Sebastian Melchior stepped out of the taxi and handed the driver his money. He stood on the sidewalk and marveled at the building in front of him.

The skyscraper.

Everyone who worked inside called it that. Technically, it was named The McCool Building, but no one used that name. Sebastian was the architect behind the tower, and he didn't call it that, either. It was just *the skyscraper* to him, too.

He was extremely proud of the project and the way it had turned out. Every floor had its own little accents and personality, but it came together as a unified whole. Form and function, married together as one. Most people probably didn't pay attention to the little things. Only someone with his background and education would appreciate the small stuff, but the skyscraper was undoubtedly unique. There wasn't another building like it anywhere in the city.

Sebastian gave the building another once over, admiring his work, and then he pushed through the front doors. The interior lobby had marble floors and a bay of elevators, shiny and bronzed. Sebastian didn't have as much say in the interior decoration choices as he did in the exterior design, but he was reasonably pleased with the look.

There were hundreds of people on the other floors, working away on their various tasks. Sebastian wasn't here to bother them, but he was going to take a stroll through a few sections of the building once he was done with his meeting.

He walked past the front desk and strode over to the bay of elevators. Pushing the call button, he stepped back and waited to see which one would light up. After a moment, the one on the far left dinged, and the doors opened. An array of buttons glowed at his fingertips. Sebastian found the floor he wanted, and the elevator lurched into motion.

The elevator went down, down, down. It didn't go up from the ground floor. There weren't any floors above the ground level.

This was one of Hell's biggest construction projects, rising from the very depths of the underworld until it pierced the crust of the surface world. From the outside, it looked like a truck depot, run down and practically invisible. Sebastian was proud of that, and he knew his meeting with the big guy on the bottom floor was going to go well. The skyscraper allowed them to reach out and pierce the upper world. Sebastian smiled to himself as he descended and the temperature grew hotter.

FIFTEEN

OCTOBER BUSINESS

Sabrina stood behind the counter and opened boxes, sorting through the new inventory. There were a few special orders that she needed to keep behind the counter. Mostly masks but a few full costumes, too.

They were all hideous.

A few of her coworkers genuinely seemed to like working here. They were the weirdos who enjoyed the grisly and the macabre. Sabrina was just here because she needed the job. The little seasonal popup shop would shut down again in a few months once Halloween was over, but it was a decent source of income until then. Mostly, she just had to keep track of the stock and refill shelves as necessary.

That didn't mean she liked it, though. She fundamentally didn't understand the people who enjoyed all this fuss. Everything in the store was grossly overpriced, and it was all ugly.

She used a boxcutter to slice open a new shipment, and she pulled out one of the special-order items she was supposed to keep behind the counter. The mask was the ugliest one yet, and it came with a set of matching gloves. Anyone wearing it would only need to wear long sleeves to transform themselves into a grotesque monster. Charming.

There were only a couple of customers inside right now, so Sabrina focused most of her attention on the task at hand. She'd look up every once in a while to make sure nobody needed help or was trying to shoplift anything. Yesterday, a kid had tried to climb one of the racks while her parents weren't looking, and Sabrina had to haul her off. She wasn't sure why anyone would take a child to a nightmare factory like this, though.

A man walked through the store's double doors, blinking in the relative darkness. He spotted Sabrina and walked over to her counter.

"Excuse me, but I placed an online order here. I got an email that said it had arrived." He held up his phone so Sabrina could see the item code.

"Of course. I just finished unpacking that," Sabrina said. This was the proud new owner of the particularly hideous mask and gloves she'd just put away. She grabbed the box and set it on the counter.

The customer opened the box and looked at the goods. He held them up, giving them a quick inspection. Sabrina had to repress a grimace as she eyed the mask again.

The mask only had a measly two eyes. There wasn't a single fang poking out of the mouth or a proboscis in sight. The fingers on the gloves were hairless and clawless.

"Here you go," Sabrina said, trying and mostly failing to hide her revulsion. The hulking, dribbling thing in front of her thanked her and took his package.

SIXTEEN
WHEN THE BELLS STRIKE TWELVE

Sheriff Ionescu stood in the middle of Redgrave's dusty street, waiting for the Wharton Gang. A few onlookers had gathered to the side, watching from windowsills and doorways with cautious curiosity.

The little Arizona town had seen its fair share of misfortune. Desperados and fraudsters of every shade, from train robbers to common snake oil salesmen, had frequented the town so often there was little left worth stealing.

The town had seen five sheriffs in the last three years. Two of them lay in the little cemetery just north of the gulch. One had resigned and ridden out of town fifteen minutes after being appointed. One had robbed the bank before disappearing. Sheriff Ionescu was the fifth and most successful lawman to come to Redgrave.

Redgrave had a terrible reputation, and it had earned it. The town attracted bandits and cutthroats the way shit attracted flies.

That was why Ionescu came here.

The townsfolk had been reluctant to let Ionescu take up the mantle of sheriff at first, but no one else within two hundred miles wanted the job. He'd won them over now that he was getting results. Ionescu had eight would-be bank robbers, all members of the Wharton Gang, stuck in the tiny jail's cells, and the number of outlaws in the cemetery was now greater than the number of ex-sheriffs.

A series of figures rode over the horizon, dust billowing up behind them. That would be Hector Wharton and his lieutenants, here to free their friends and no doubt exact revenge on Redgrave and its sheriff. As they drew closer, Ionescu could see the glint of gunmetal.

They were right on time. Ionescu had invited them here as part of a simple challenge. It was a variation on a classic. A duel. Just Ionescu and Hector Wharton and a dusty, western street. As soon as the bell tower chimed twelve o'clock, they would do their level best to kill each other.

This was why Ionescu came here.

Hector Wharton and his henchmen slowed dismounted. A couple of them spat out streams of tobacco juice. All of them held pistols, rifles, or shotguns. No one was waiting to unholster anything.

"You came," Ionescu said. "You know the terms. Standard rules. Wait until the bells chime twelve, and then we duel."

"I'm not waiting for any of that crap. Kill 'im, boys," Wharton said. A fusillade of gunfire rang out, bullets striking Ionescu from several angles at once. A shotgun blast blew his body out of his boots, knocking him down to the ground. The townspeople who had come to watch flinched away.

Right on time, the clock struck midnight, and Ionescu picked himself back up. His fangs flashed in the moonlight as he walked toward the startled outlaws.

This was why Ionescu came here. An endless supply of fresh blood from people who wouldn't be missed, and a town that was happy to protect his coffin while he slept through the daylight hours.

<u>SEVENTEEN</u>
PUBLIC DEFENDER

"We find the defendant guilty on all counts," the lead juror said, his voice forceful. They'd only deliberated for two hours, which was a very short period of time to talk about some sixteen murders.

Derek Miller placed his hands over his face and quietly wept as the bailiff stepped in to take him away. The camera crews from the local news stations zoomed in as the condemned man's public defender leaned over and patted Derek on the back.

Seamus Langley watched as his client was taken away amid an explosion of flashbulbs. A few of the cameras turned to him as he made his way out of the court room. He said a few brief words in response to the shouted questions.

"Of course we'll appeal. It was a deeply flawed process. Yes, yes, my client's innocence will be proven in time." Seamus waved most of the questions away. He didn't want to deal with any of it right now.

He walked down the hallway, a file of papers under his arm, loosening his necktie with his free hand. A couple of prosecutors spotted him. They nodded at him. The news would be all over the courthouse by now.

Derek Miller had just been found guilty of butchering sixteen women with a hatchet. He took their eyes after each slaying, apparently scooping them right out with a melon baller. His DNA, mostly from stray hairs, had been found at most of the scenes. Two more murders were officially unsolved, but the police suspected Derek was involved. Seamus probably never had a chance in the courtroom. From the moment *voir dire* ended and the jury was selected, Seamus and Derek were probably screwed.

Seamus had represented Derek before. Derek was a frequent flyer with the local jail, usually for driving while intoxicated or dumb misdemeanors. No one saw the murderer behind Derek's dull, piggish eyes, though.

Walking down to the public defender's office in the bottom of the courthouse, Seamus sat down at his desk and pawed through the stack of cases that had landed on his desk in just the last few hours.

The file on top belonged to one Terrence "Snakebite" Jones. He was another name Seamus was familiar with. A couple hold ups. Petty larceny. Urinating in public. A lot.

Seamus reached into his desk drawer and pulled out the little baggie of Snakebite's hair. He also had fibers from a couple of the man's jackets. And a little vial of spit, carefully swabbed off the floor the last time Snakebite graced Seamus with his presence.

Snakebite was another client Seamus genuinely did not like. Like all the others, he was a couple crayons short of a rainbow. But more importantly, he was annoying.

Seamus would have to come up with a new modus operandi. Maybe a hammer serial killer. Maybe a strangler. Seamus had some time to think about it. With Snakebite assigned to his docket, Seamus would know his schedule, though. He'd know when he did and didn't have an alibi. And he'd already surreptitiously collected all the evidence he needed. Soon, he'd once more be rid of another obnoxious client.

EIGHTEEN
CRYPTO-BOTANY

Dr. Alfonse Herringstadt moved through the jungle. This was one of the last, truly undisturbed corners of the world, where the vines ran rampant and the plant life grew in a green riot.

For a crypto-botanist like himself, it was heaven. For everyone else, it was a verdant hell. The jungle was stiflingly hot, and the air was pregnant with cloying moisture. Sweat popped out on Alfonse's skin just from trying to move down the game trail. He constantly had to be on the lookout for camouflaged vipers and spiders big enough to eat a puppy.

The biggest problem was trying to stay dry. Aside from just his own sweat, he had to ford muddy streams and shelter through torrential rain storms. They didn't call it a rain forest for nothing. He knew from experience that the jungle was even more miserable when he was soaked to the bone. Squelching around in wet socks and chafing underwear was a special kind of misery in this sticky, syrupy heat.

He could tell from the way the air hung around him like a mildewing blanket that another storm was brewing. He'd have to find a spot to shelter soon, because he wouldn't make it back to the tent at this rate.

It wasn't a pleasant trek, but he was in his element. Discovering new species of plants was his great passion in life. Some of them were previously thought extinct. Others had legendary medicinal properties that had been forgotten by everyone but indigenous tribes. Others were simply beautiful. He now had two species of orchid named in his honor, which he was extremely proud of.

However, he hadn't found his white whale yet. There was one particular plant species that he'd always searched for but never seen. Once or twice, he'd heard whispers about it, but the trail always seemed to run cold. Maybe this time, he'd capture the proof he'd been looking for.

A fat raindrop fell out of the sky, splashed off a canopy leaf overhead, and landed on the back of Alfonse's neck. More quickly followed. He scurried along, moving as fast as he dared through the rough terrain, but soon the path ahead of him was lost in the downpour. His glasses fogged up in the warm rain, and he stumbled onward, searching for the first bit of shelter he could find.

There! He spotted a tree with a gigantic set of leaves, each one shaped roughly like the two lobes of a fish's tail. They were sufficiently large to turn the rain and keep him dry.

Alfonse lunged into the dry space and shook himself off. Wiping his glasses clear of the raindrops, he looked up at the tree sheltering him.

Wait. No. Could it be? Alfonse blinked. He wasn't sheltering under a tree at all. He'd found it. His white whale! It was real, and he'd finally discovered it! This was amazing. And bad. Very bad.

Alfonse tried to run, but he tripped on a rock laying on the ground. No, not a rock. Bone.

Then, the mouth of the gargantuan Venus Flytrap bent over him, and the lobe-shaped leaves clamped shut.

NINETEEN

HOG FARM

Chris wiped the knife off on his rubberized apron. The pig was dead. It had finally stopped twitching and squirming. Evidently his aim had been a little bit off.

He always used a .22 pistol to put hogs down and start the butchering process. The trick was to aim in between the eyes and just a little up. That would normally let them off nice and quick, with minimal muss and fuss for everyone involved. This one had more fight in it, though. It had taken a few rounds to shove the animal off this mortal coil.

Grabbing some rope and his winch, he hoisted the pig up by its back legs. He'd have to drain the animal's blood, clean it, and skin it before it was ready. Then he'd have to pull the offal out and all the other preparations before the animal was ready for eating. He didn't particularly enjoy this process, but it put food on his table.

His little farm on the edge of Furnace Plains, Kansas had to provide him with everything. A lot of his food came right from his land and anything else he needed, be it gas for his car or a new book for his shelf, was paid for with the bounty from his land.

He was pushing the edge of his budget with these pigs, though. They weren't his. Not originally, anyway. After Kelley McCabe from south end of the county disappeared, up and vanished without a trace, his land and hogs had gone on the auction block. People talked about what had happened to McCabe. Won the lottery and ran away to Tahiti. Got offed by the mob. Aliens.

Chris didn't know. He barely knew McCabe. Didn't particularly care for the man, though. With his big, gold tooth and that smug grin he always wore, the man struck Chris as too slick for his own good. If he was a wagering man, he would have gone with the mob theory.

Maybe McCabe wasn't his favorite person, but he couldn't pass up that lot of McCabe's hogs when they went under the gavel. They were big, fat beasts. Chris would just have to keep them fed and penned for a few weeks before they were ready to be sent off to market. It had seemed like the deal of a lifetime, and he'd snatched it up. A couple of the hogs would go in his freezer and feed his family, but the rest would go straight into his pocketbook.

He tried to think about what he could do with the extra money, instead of what his hands were doing inside the dead hog. A new roof for the barn. Fixing the fence by the drive. Maybe a puppy for Lucinda.

His hand touched something that didn't feel right, and he snapped out of his happy little daydream. Digging around, he slit part of the hog's belly open. Bile and blood sluiced out, but something clattered to the floor. It was a shiny little speck, something made of metal.

Chris bent down and picked it up, flicking some of the nasty juices off. It was a tooth. A glittering, gold tooth. The implications took a second to tick through Chris's brain.

He turned around. He needed to get back to the house and call the sheriff.

The pigs were blocking his way. They stood in the doorway, silent. Some of them stared at the butchered hog hanging from the winch. Others were staring at Chris. As if by some unspoken signal, they began to move toward him.

TWENTY
HUNGRY, HUNGRY

Susan walked across the field to Mr. Beardsley's farmhouse. It was a beautiful spring day, and she enjoyed the feel of the warm sunlight on her skin. A butterfly flitted past, carried along by the breeze.

Mr. Beardsley sold antiques out of his house. The old man had a considerable amount of old junk sitting around from when he was younger and the land a lot more profitable. Susan liked to peruse the old items, picking out odds and ends to serve as accent pieces.

She noticed that the small plot of land that Mr. Beardsley still worked had been harvested. He'd done that remarkably fast. When she drove by a week ago, his personal garden had been bursting with corn and tomatoes and bean stalks. Now, it looked like he'd taken virtually everything out. There wasn't much left except dirt in the little fenced in garden.

Another butterfly danced past Susan's head as she reached the main walkway and started toward the house. Mr. Beardsley had cleared a lot of the vegetation and debris away from his home, too. Last year, she'd helped him clear some of the weeds and brush that crept up too close to the house. They'd become friends over the years, and she liked to give him a hand every now and then. Sometimes, they'd even just sit out in the garden and enjoy some coffee together.

He must have hired someone to clear the yard debris this year, though. Susan actually felt a little disappointed. It wasn't that she was looking forward to hacking away at blackberry briars and overgrown weeds, but she hadn't even gotten a chance to ask if he wanted a hand this year. Did he think she didn't want to help anymore? She racked her brain, trying to think if she'd said anything the last time she was here that could be construed that way.

A couple more butterflies flapped past. Susan stopped to admire them, and one landed on her arm. She stood very still for a moment, wondering if the butterfly would move if she reached for her camera. She wanted a picture, if she could get one.

But then a thought occurred to her. What if something happened to Mr. Beardsley? She wouldn't necessarily know. She wasn't family. She wouldn't be on any contact list if he was hospitalized. If something had happened, his adult children might have hired someone to clean the place up. She forgot the butterfly and started toward the front porch again.

Looking around, she saw that it wasn't just the brush that had been cleared around the house. Most of the lawn was gone. But she didn't see shovel marks or churned dirt. It was like the grass had evaporated. And the trees, which should have been covered in budding leaves, were completely barren. The forest at the edge of Mr. Beardsley's property looked sickly and unwelcoming for this time of year.

Walking faster, Susan stepped up onto the porch and knocked. Another butterfly landed on her, alighting onto her hair this time. She knocked. No one answered. She knocked again. Silence.

Shifting over to the window, Susan pressed her face to the glass, cupping her hands to block the sunlight. She didn't see anyone inside. Just as she was about to turn around and try knocking again, she spotted a pair of pantlegs near the far side of the porch. There was a pair of boots at the ends of the legs.

A sudden dread filling her heart, Susan walked to the edge of the porch and poked her head around. The skeletonized body lay in the bare dirt, the bones sitting under the open sky. Mr. Beardsley's favorite hat lay nearby, tattered and frayed.

The body was covered in caterpillars. They writhed on the clothes, nibbling at the fabric. The seethed across the bones, squirming in and out of the skull. They devoured the few remaining plant stalks near the corpse.

Susan stood in shocked silence for a moment. An odd sensation on her arm snapped her out of it. There was warm liquid on her arm. She looked down and saw blood, a shocking amount of blood. The butterfly that landed on her arm hadn't left when she started moving again. Now, it had its proboscis buried in her arm, sucking greedily. She felt a little bolt of pain on her scalp, where the other butterfly had attached itself to her hair. Susan staggered off the porch and ran as more butterflies started to emerge from the woods, flapping toward her.

TWENTY-ONE

TERMINAL

Neil Tucker typed a message to his girlfriend, Samantha. He'd been so busy finishing up his doctorate in computer sciences and electrical engineering, that he hadn't been able to just relax with her in what felt like forever. He wouldn't have been able to make it this far without her.

He stared at the message for a moment and rubbed his eyes. It was late, and he was still in the lab. The good news was, he was finally done with his project. He'd spent years on it now, and he'd relied on Samantha through all of it.

Right now, he just wanted to be with her. He was tired but proud. The computing system he'd developed was a next generation processor that could handle a huge amount of data at once. If it made it through all its tests, he'd be able to sell the rights and design to the highest bidder. He planned to keep the prototype, though. It had sentimental value at this point, and it still had a few minor design flaws that needed to be ironed out.

Samantha messaged him back, the text flashing up on his screen. "Does this mean you're done with the project?"

He typed back. "More or less. There's a couple little things that I need to tweak, but the important stuff is all finished. Then, it's just me and you, babe." He stuck a little heart icon at the end of the message.

Neil had always loved her for her mind. She was a fellow computer science student when they first met. She hadn't worked directly on the new processing system. She hadn't drawn up the designs and soldered everything together anyway, but she still deserved a heap of credit. He couldn't have gotten as far as he did without her. She was his muse.

Someone walked down the hallway, their shoes clicking on the tile floor. The noise was loud in the otherwise abandoned lab. Neil threw a sheet over his project. Perhaps he was just paranoid, but now that the bulk of the work was done, he didn't want anybody getting nosy until everything was officially ready to unveil. He doubted anyone could come close to copying what he'd done in that small amount of time, but he still didn't want one of the professors or his fellow engineers to barge in on him before he was ready.

The computer beeped, and a new message popped up on screen.

Neil didn't look at it right away. He eyed the doorway until he saw one of the night custodians walk past. The man waved to him, and he nodded back. He pulled the sheet back off, revealing the glass tank with the brain inside. Wires and electrodes poked out of the wrinkly, gray mass, connecting to various inputs. He checked Samantha's message.

"If you're done, then end my suffering. Kill me, Neil. Kill me."

He typed back. "And ruin your big debut? I couldn't do that to you, sweetie." He added a little winking emoji.

TWENTY-TWO

QUESTIONS FOR A MARINE BIOLOGIST

Dr. Amy Jackson stood on the beach, eyeing the sight in front of her. She wiped her brow, smearing sweat and old sunscreen away. She and her team had already been out here for hours, and things weren't getting any better. In fact, they were getting worse.

Two of the pilot whales they'd managed to drag off the sand had immediately flung themselves back onto the beach. There were nearly three dozen of the small whales stuck on the beach now, and they were in trouble.

Amy's team was split up in a variety of tasks. Some had nets and pallets, and they were doing everything they could to drag the animals back into the water. Others were walking among the still stranded animals and hosing them down as best as possible. A few people had the unenviable task of performing triage, trying to figure out which of the animals they had time to save and which they'd have to let die. There were simply too many of them, and some of them were in a better position to survive than others, but only if Amy's team worked fast and efficiently.

And only if the whales stopped heaving themselves back onto land. No one knew exactly why whales would commit to mass beachings. There was some evidence that military-grade sonar disoriented them and could accidentally send them to land. Sometimes a single old or diseased whale might become confused and strand itself, and the others would follow its sounds of distress, accidentally trapping themselves, too. Sometimes a toxic algae bloom or an oil spill would force them into shallow water. Other times, a lack of food might do the same.

Amy had spent her life studying the phenomenon. Even when she was a little girl, she loved whales. Their huge size and majesty fascinated her then, and put her on the path to becoming a marine biologist.

Twenty years and a divorce later, she wasn't any closer to understanding what drove whales onto land than when she started her studies. It was always heartbreaking, though. She took another swig of water and waded back into the middle of the stranded pod of whales. Why would otherwise intelligent creatures with a built-in suite of navigation tools end up stranding themselves? It was a life-long question that still bothered her.

Suddenly, an answer presented itself as a massive tentacle rose up out of the water and grabbed one of the volunteers pushing a whale into the water. Another tentacle and then another emerged from the surf and surged forward, snatching up anything that moved, dragging it into the sea and toward a giant, gnashing beak.

TWENTY-THREE

ROAMING

Daniel walked in to find Kayla talking on his cellphone. The bulky, scratched phone looked gigantic in her little hands. It was adorable, but she was supposed to know not to use his phone without asking permission first.

"Who ya' talking to, Sweetie?" Daniel asked, using his Dad voice. Not unfriendly but stern.

"Mommy's on the phone," Kayla said, happy as could be.

That hit Daniel hard. It almost doubled him over. That wasn't what he was expecting to hear. That wasn't what he was expecting to hear at all. He put on a tough face, though.

"You know Mommy's…gone," he said.

"But she's right here." Kayla held the phone up so Daniel could see. The screen was black, and the same old cracks ran across one section of the screen where he'd dropped the damn thing.

"We talked about this," Daniel said. He sighed and went down on his knees beside Kayla. "It's like what happened with Bowie. Remember how he went away to a better place?"

Kayla nodded.

Bowie had been Daniel and Shelby's dog. His full name wasn't Bowie but rather Duke Boleslaw of Bohemia, Protector of Moravia. That was what Daniel got for marrying a medieval history nerd. Bowie was a spazz, but Daniel had loved that little dog. Shelby got him right before she and Daniel met. Kayla loved Bowie too, although she was too young to remember him very well at this point. That had been her first brush with death. Daniel would have done anything to make sure it was her last.

Daniel looked at his daughter. He didn't want to punish her for trying to contact her mother. That wouldn't be right. But he couldn't allow this to continue any further, either. That wouldn't be healthy for anyone. Still, he couldn't help himself.

"Did Mommy say anything to you?"

"She wouldn't stop crying," Kayla said, sounding suddenly sad. "I'm worried about her."

47

"Let's worry about us for now," Daniel said, gently plucking his cracked phone out of Kayla's hands. He sat down and stared at the partially busted phone.

He didn't know how Kayla sometimes managed to get service in this purgatory. The phone shouldn't even work. Just like him and Kayla, it had been smashed pretty hard in the car accident.

***

Shelby sat in the driver's seat but didn't start the car. She kept staring at her phone, willing it to ring again, willing it to prove she wasn't crazy. She was still in the funeral parlor's parking lot. The urns, both the big one and the small one, were strapped into the child seat in the back. It was macabre, but it seemed like the safest place for them, and she hadn't had the energy or the will power to take the seat out yet.

That was when the phone rang. An unidentified number. And her daughter's voice as dry and distant as next autumn's leaves had come through the speaker. This wasn't the first time this had happened, but she hoped it was the last. Or that it would continue all the time. Her daughter's voice…

Shelby sat in the car and trembled, waiting and waiting.

TWENTY-FOUR

THE MARY-ANNE

"Throttle up a bit," Captain Prenzer said.

"Propulsion, give us some gas." His executive officer echoed the command down the chain.

The vessel slid forward, nice and easy, just the way Prenzer wanted. This was a stealth mission. He couldn't afford to cause undue commotion. In just a few short moments, they'd either be in the clear and past the enemy defenses, or they'd be spotted, and everyone would probably die horribly.

Prenzer maintained a calm, cool demeanor. Imperious, even. If he looked like he believed victory was assured, his underlings would believe it, too. Truth be told though, he wasn't at all sure how this was going to turn out.

He'd been with Task Force Six practically forever, but this was his first genuine command position. Working his way up the ranks paid off, though. And if he succeeded with this plan, he and his crew would be heroes back home. There'd be a commendation in order and plenty more prestigious postings than the *Mary-Anne*.

Prenzer liked his vessel, the *Mary-Anne*, though. She was slow and creaky and built up fumes like nobody's business, but she was all his. As far as he was concerned, she was his finest possession. Even if she wasn't much to look at, Prenzer knew the old girl could do some damage under the right circumstances. He'd just spent the last three months trying to engineer those circumstances.

Now, the moment of truth had arrived. He held his breath as they came up to the line of outer contact. He glanced at his executive officer and nodded.

"Just like we practiced, Damien."

Sister Mary-Anne Stimpson stopped in front of the guard at the Vatican gate and handed him her identification.

The man glanced at the little plastic ID and waved her through. If he noticed that her eyes were too red or her jerky, marionette movements or the off-putting smell, he didn't say anything. The elderly nun crossed the threshold without a word.

They were in. All around him, Prenzer's host of demonic minions cheered. Their stealth possession mission had gone off without a hitch.

"Give 'em hell, Captain."

Listen, please. You have to help me. My name is George. I'm pretty sure that I'm a character in one of these stories. I can see what's been happening, and if you read my story, I'll probably die. Please stop reading.

TWENTY-FIVE

WALLFLOWERS

Josie fidgeted with her wool sweater. She purchased the reindeer-festooned garment at the thrift store. Scrounging through the rack of lovingly knitted but hastily donated Christmas outfits, she always felt guilty buying up attire meant for those less fortunate than herself. Still, there was no sense wrecking nice clothes during the transformation.

The final guest stood. "I'm Todd, and I'm a werewolf."

"Hi, Todd," everyone responded. Josie liked Todd. He seemed like a sweet guy. Still, she refused to date anyone inside the group.

Ella made that mistake with Warren. After she had that litter of jackals with him, the town hunted them both down and with torches and silver bullets. A pity. They were such a cute couple, too.

"Alright," Josie rose from her seat, "I'm glad everybody could make it to our monthly meeting." She started to pack the refreshments while everyone mingled, waiting for nightfall.

"Sorry if my basement is a little cramped."

"No, it's perfect. Thanks for hosting," Todd said, getting up to load leftover casserole into baggies with her. "Nobody will barge in on us down here, and you prepared some great food."

"It's nothing."

"No really. It's not like we can order out," Todd laughed. "You really outdid yourself with the snacks. We'd get snappy with each other if not for your spread over there," he gestured to the three figures manacled to the wall, their eyes bulging in terror over their gags.

Her teeth glinted as she smiled at Todd.

You haven't stopped reading. I know. It sounds insane, but it's true. It sounds like some sort of gimmick, but it's my reality. All these people, the ones who've died, that was real to them, too. Just stop reading.

<u>TWENTY-SIX</u>
CAMPFIRE STORIES

"Do you guys want to hear a scary story?" Tom asked, holding the flashlight under his chin. The fire popped and crackled. Young Johnny had a marshmallow on a stick. His older sister, Rosie, was working on a length of severely blackened sausage.

"Tom, don't," Barb said. His wife hated every aspect of camping, even if it was a family tradition. She scratched at a bug bite on her arm.

It was too late, though. Tom had Johnny and Rosie's attention now.

"Once, in these very woods, there was a summer camp," Tom said, channeling every ounce of drama he could muster.

"Where?" Johnny asked, his marshmallow catching fire as his attention focused on Tom.

"Down by the lake, less than a mile from here."

"Tom, don't scare them," Barb said.

"But they *need* to hear this," Tom said. "Their lives could depend on it." He waved his hands for effect.

Rosie, who was old enough to ignore him a lot of the time these days, took a little bite of her food, but her eyes were glued to her father. She'd heard this same story on last year's trip, when Johnny was still too young to remember. Some stories never got old, though.

"The camp counselors tried to play a prank on some of the kids, and they threw fire crackers in one of the cabins, planning to scare the campers awake. But the fireworks started a blaze, and a young boy and a girl, not so very different from your ages, were horribly burned."

Johnny's eyes were wide now. His son might not be sleeping tonight.

"Years later, when the camp reopened after the lawsuits, the counselors came early for training. But they didn't know a maniac was in the woods, waiting for them. One by one, the campers fell, until there was only one left. She ran through the woods and hid in this very campground. But the maniac wasn't done yet."

Now Rosie was looking around, watching the darkness around the fire. Tom loved this story.

"The last counselor didn't count on a *second* maniac, the other burned child from all those years ago. The next day, the police found all the counselors' heads lined up by the lake, but the bodies had all been burned."

"Tom…" Barb was giving him a dirty look now. Time to wrap up.

"Anyway, that's what your mother and I did on our honeymoon, and we've been back every year since. Time to get to get some sleep, buckos. Camp opens tomorrow."

Tom finished sharpening his machete and held it up in his burned, scarred hands.

You've probably read about parallel universes or multi-verses or whatever fancy name you prefer in science fiction. It's in movies. I've seen them. Yeah, the Avengers and stuff? We have that, too. We're all happily living our lives, just trying to get by. We are alive, dammit. But every time you read another story, something awful happens. Put the book down. Refund it. Throw it away.

TWENTY-SEVEN
DONATED TO SCIENCE

Franklin sat down at his desk in the symposium room and wrinkled his nose.

A few smells competed for dominance in the classroom. There was the odor of lemon antiseptic cleaner, which was ubiquitous throughout the medical college. But there was also the smell of death and rot, as if a refrigerator in the grocer's meat section had lost power. It was pungent and cloying. Franklin hadn't noticed it until he sat down.

Oh no.

"Good morning, students. Today you will mark one of the most important moments in your medical training. I have a number of human cadavers here, donated to science by the recently deceased, and I will help you dissect and catalog their components today," Dr. Raskin said.

Several of the other medical students looked around at each other, a sudden anxiety in their eyes. A couple feigned nonchalance, but they also glanced around. One or two people didn't seem at all phased by this news, their poker faces completely unreadable. Jason, Franklin's personal rival and a grade-A jerk, was among that group. Franklin had read once that the medical profession had a disproportionate number of sociopaths.

Dr. Raskin wheeled a gurney out to the center of the classroom. A blanket lay over the gurney, an unmistakable shape beneath. The smell grew a little stronger.

Jason raised his hand but didn't wait for Dr. Raskin to acknowledge him. "Is there supposed to be such a strong smell?"

Dr. Raskin looked up and adjusted his glasses. "To be perfectly honest, I hadn't noticed it until just now. This would be a good opportunity to bring up my most important lesson of the day, though. Respect. These people agreed to bare their deepest secrets to us. It will be very personal and sometimes rather unpleasant. You're not used to this yet, and it may provoke some laughter out of you. That's fine today. Sometimes people get the nervous giggles.

However, you will not have that luxury once you leave this institution. These are real people who donated their bodies, and this was a selfless act on their part. You might find yourself giving a surprised chortle as we get into the gross stuff today, and I'll forgive that. But if I hear any rude or disparaging comments from someone who fancies himself a joker, I'll destroy you. Got it?"

Franklin liked Dr. Raskin, but he suddenly knew he wasn't going to make it all the way through this lesson. That smell.

Someone near the front raised her hand. "May I be excused for a moment? I need some fresh air."

Dr. Raskin nodded. "Good idea. Anyone else who needs to step out at any time, do it. Ask to look at someone else's notes later. We don't need anyone getting sick in here."

Franklin knew this was his opportunity. He hastily got up out of his seat, that smell seemingly swirling around him. He shuffled his way to the end of the row and hastily made his way out into the hallway and down to the bathroom. The odor followed him outside, clinging to everything.

He ran into a stall and lifted up his shirt. There was a rupture in his skin suit. One line of stitches had burst, revealing the dead, rotten flesh below. The smell intensified inside the bathroom. Damn. Damn, damn, damn.

It had been almost two months since he escaped from Dr. Raskin's laboratory. So far, the professor seemed to have no idea that his missing creation had returned. The professor, effectively Franklin's father, wouldn't acknowledge what had happened, but Franklin had to return, albeit in disguise. If Franklin could just get close to the professor, he could learn the techniques to fix himself properly. Until then, he just needed to excise a patch of flesh to patch himself up like a tire.

Jason walked into the room and started washing his hands. Franklin came up behind him, scalpel in hand.

Every time you read one of these, something terrible happens. This is all real to us. We might not exist on the exact same plane of existence you do, but that doesn't make it any less real to us.

TWENTY-EIGHT
SANDY BEACHES

Max pushed his way through the jungle and emerged at the edge of the beach. He was sweaty and tired, and he was pretty sure that he had a weird bug bite now. But maybe it was worth it.

He hadn't been at all satisfied with the beach by the hotel. It was crowded with tourists and screaming kids and abandoned trash. The pamphlets had promised pristine, white beaches on the edge of paradise. Instead, it was just another tourist trap.

Max didn't come here to vacation with every idiot in the Caribbean. He'd asked the hotel staff about different beaches. They'd told him to stay on the shore next to the hotel. He'd asked the local restaurant staff about different beaches. They'd told him to stay on the shore next to the hotel. He'd asked the taxi driver about different beaches, and he finally got an answer he wanted.

All he had to do was hike over the ridge, fighting his way through the underbrush, and he was there. The driver said that no one really used the beach over there. Too much hassle to get there. Something about the locals not liking the place. Max had a hard time understanding the driver's accent, but he got what he needed.

And this was exactly what he needed. He looked around the empty beach. The sand was almost pure white, with yellowish undertones. It was pebbly under his boots, crunching with each step he took toward the water. It looked like a lot of it was crushed sea shells rather than sand. That was why the beach had such a distinct, creamy color.

He had the whole place to himself. Not another soul to be seen. The trek through the snarl of vines and trees was worth it. First thing first. He pulled out his camera and took a few shots, including some selfies. These were going on social media later. Hell yeah. All his friends could seethe with envy for a few hours while he enjoyed paradise.

Heading toward the water, he pulled a towel and some beer out of his pack. The beach was actually getting grittier the closer he got to the water, the seashell sand coming in bigger chunks. At the edge of the jungle, it was little more than silt and pebbles. It was more like gravel at the edge of the ocean, though.

Max spotted some larger stones, all of them oddly shaped. He walked past some kelp-covered driftwood, and noticed the same, eggshell color on the wood. He had nearly slugged back the entirety of the first can of beer when he tripped on a particularly large rock, mostly buried in the sand.

He looked back and realized it wasn't a rock he'd tripped on. It was a skull. A human skull. The domed part of the head stuck out above the rest of the pebbly sand. From the back, it just looked like another rock. From this side, he could see the eye sockets, half-buried in the pebbles. A crab scuttled out of one of the empty eyes.

Max had a realization. The pebbly grit strewn across the beach was the same off-white color as the sun-bleached skull. He wasn't walking across crushed seashells. They were crumbled bones. Those weren't pieces of driftwood caught in the kelp. They were femurs and scapulas. The whole beach was strewn with pale death.

Max turned around to run back to the hotel. That was when he saw the figures emerging from the jungle behind him. The dark shapes, twisted and inhuman, closed in.

These stories, they're already written, but things don't transpire until you actually read them. It's like the observer's paradox. Having an observer triggers certain conditions. You are unwittingly causing all these things to happen. Some of them are merely unpleasant. A lot have been deadly.

If you stop reading, we live. Keep reading,
and we die.

TWENTY-NINE
QUANTITY HAS A QUALITY ALL ITS OWN

Sheriff Donahue kicked the door to the professor's laboratory in. The lock broke free, and the door flung inward in a burst of splinters. Donahue was here to arrest Dr. Herman Everdeen for his crimes. But it was also his job to make sure that the crowd outside didn't tear Everdeen apart before he ever saw the inside of a jail cell. The deputies were out front, keeping the angry mob at bay. Even above the sounds of the crowd, Donahue could hear the storm raging outside.

Donahue had been investigating the series of grave robberies afflicting the town. No one wanted to bury their loved ones anymore for fear that the bodies would be dug up and taken away, sometimes mere hours after the funeral. It wasn't just a problem in town, either. The little burgs on the county's outskirts had experienced the same thing. There'd been spotty reports from all over the southern half of the state. Donahue didn't have enough men to post on twenty-four hour guard duty at every churchyard and cemetery, though.

But Professor Everdeen had finally overplayed his hand. Donahue had the evidence he needed to nail the sick son of a bitch. A lot of people had laid suspicion at Everdeen's feet. The retired doctor was known as something of a kook, with an interest in unconventional medicine. Donahue had arranged to run into him a couple of times in town and tried to pump him for information, but he'd come back dry each time. Now, he had Everdeen, though.

The professor stood in the middle of his laboratory, standing over a slab with a shroud over it. There was a distinctly human shape beneath the shroud. A lightning rod poked out through a hole in the ceiling, and buzzing machinery of every description lines the walls.

"It's over, Everdeen. I know what you've been up to. Step away from the equipment and come with me," Donahue ordered.

"I'm afraid I'm rather busy right now," Everdeen said, his hand on the lever of one of the machines.

"I don't have time to play games with you. You can come with me, or I can throw you to the crowd," Donahue said as lightning crackled overhead.

Outside, he could still hear screaming and shouting. A gun shot rang out. Donahue dearly hoped that was one of his men firing a warning shot, and not the beginning of an armed brawl. He didn't have much time to bring the local mad scientist into custody safely.

"And just what is it you accuse me of?"

"Grave robbery. You've been stealing bodies and using the best parts for your research. I've read *Frankenstein*. It's obvious what you're up to at this point."

"Ah, but I'm afraid you're wrong, Sheriff," Everdeen said.

It was then that the far wall smashed inward. A massive, hunched figure stood in the opening, dripping with rain water. Nearly thirty feet tall and covered from head to toe with stitches, it was barely recognizable as anything that had ever been human. It held the limp body of one of Donahue's deputies in one meaty paw and a member of the mob in the other. It tossed them away like toys and turned its beady, piggish eyes on Donahue.

"I haven't been using the best parts from the bodies," Professor Everdeen said. "I've been using *all* the parts."

The massive creature turned and reached for Donahue.

Fine. I see that you have chosen to actively work against me and everyone else at this point. I have some access to the files. I'll force you to stop. I'm starting this whole thing over. You don't have a choice but to stop now.

<u>ONE</u>
GENTLY USED

I stood in the middle of the lot, near a giant, inflatable gorilla. I must have been gawping at the merchandise because a salesman sidled up to me.

The kid looked like he'd just graduated, and his face was fighting a war of attrition with acne. The acne was winning.

"It's time for Big Mike's annual April sale. We're overflowing with deals on selected inventory. Be sure to check out our Dealer's Choice item. We'd have to be crazy to have such low prices," he rattled off a spiel that he'd no doubt memorized from a notecard.

"Give me the skinny on the Dealer's Choice." We started walking to another section of the lot.

"GEORGE, YOUR TIME HAS COME. I WILL FIND YOU AND DESTROY YOU ONCE AND FOR ALL." The salesman's skin started to dribble off his body like hot tallow, running down his cheap suit in greasy rivulets.

"Little old lady only used it once. Never heard that before." What turnip truck did he think I just fell off of?

The salesman bent backwards at a ninety-degree angle, his spine cracking like someone sat on a bag of potato chips. The puddle of melted skin near his feet began to reform itself into a new and terrible shape.

"IT WILL BE SWIFT. PAINLESS. CEASE YOUR STRUGGLE. I CAN BE GENTLE. OR I CAN CRUSH YOU LIKE A BEACHED WHALE ASPHYXIATING UNDER ITS OWN WEIGHT. BUT YOU WILL BE MINE, GEORGE. YOU CANNOT ESCAPE," the half-formed polypus mass of skin and blood said.

"What're your pricing options?"

The salesman's body sucked in on itself like an overburdened trash bag ripping and spilling its contents across the floor. The man's bones snapped and rearranged themselves into a new, spider-like shape. The creature skittered forward, dragging its melting innards behind it like a long, pink tail.

"Mind opening it up? I wanna check the interior."

The thing, the hideous, godawful thing skittered up to the Model DT-10 and wrenched the door off with its freakish, bloodied claws.

"There's some scratch marks on the interior upholstery. That knock the price down any further?"

"YOUR FATE AWAITS YOU, GEORGE. THIS SHALL BE YOUR RESTING PLACE," the bubbling wad of muscle and bone wheezed, gesturing at the open coffin. Then, it clattered away.

I started to follow him past the Big Mike's Gently Used Coffins sign toward the showroom.

Oh. Oh, shit.

THIRTY

COVERED WAGONS

The covered wagons ground their way through the dust. The shortcut they'd taken had been anything but. Everyone in the wagon train was supposed to arrive in California weeks ago.

Winston had given up on asking his father when they were supposed to reach their destination. Father didn't even acknowledge the question anymore. He'd grown sullen and quiet since they had to leave Old Man Crenshaw behind.

Father was in charge of the wagon train, which meant it was his fault they had taken this route. They'd taken the cutoff through the mountains, which had put them in the middle of a thicket, forcing them to chop their own path. Now, they found themselves in a desert basin. Their water and food supplies were running perilously low.

Old Man Crenshaw had been the slowest wagon, even when they were still on time. The old man, always wearing his tall stovepipe hat, had equally old oxen pulling his wagon. He usually lagged behind the rest of the train, catching up to their campfires after night had fallen. Winston liked Old Man Crenshaw, though. He'd always tell Winston about the little cabin he intended to build on the California coast, watching the waves and popping ground squirrels for a nightly stew. He also told Winston stories about what it was like to work as a frontier lumberjack, back in the days when Missouri was the edge of the world.

But they were so far behind schedule, and the other caravanners were already starting to grumble before the axle broke on Crenshaw's wagon. They'd tried to repair it for him, but no one had the right equipment or tools. None that they could spare anyway. No one wanted to give up what they would need to survive, if the same thing happened to them.

So, they'd left him with some of their dwindling water supplies and told Old Man Crenshaw that they'd come back for him, assuming no one else came along the trail and picked him up.

But Winston knew no one would collect Old Man Crenshaw. This wagon train carved this trail, and they were well off the beaten path. The water supply they left behind wouldn't last a week, even if Old Man Crenshaw let his oxen run free to die in the desert.

That had been ten days ago.

Father sat in the front of the wagon, urging their oxen to go faster through the hot, hot sands. He hadn't said a word since yesterday.

The oxen were tired. Dust hung in the air, making it hard to breathe. The heat sent shimmers across the pack dirt behind them.

Those shimmers almost hid the figure gaining on them from behind, sometimes walking, sometimes loping along on all fours, jittering and twitching like a frog with a current run through it. And they couldn't hide the fact that it was steadily gaining on them. Or the stovepipe hat perched on the figure's head.

Father urged the weakening oxen forward, but Winston knew they would have to stop soon.

THIRTY-ONE

EARWORM

Dr. Shandra Vijayakanth had spent the last eight years working in the military's sonic weapons department. It was an obscure little corner that existed within the Department of Defense. There were only a few researchers on staff.

She'd worked on a variety of projects, with varying degrees of success. The Long Range Acoustic Device, loving known as the LRAD, was one of her babies. Shandra's LRAD produced a powerful wave of ultra high-pitched sound which could be directed over a significant distance. The noise it produced was well above the pain threshold of the average person. A few naval vessels had them to discourage smaller boats from approaching. As soon as anything got close, it would be blasted with a crippling wave of noise.

There were other projects she'd worked on as well. Using certain frequencies could produce different effects, because they would harmonize in different ways. There was the legendary Brown Note, which used resonance within the human body to cause subjects to lose control of their bowels the same way some opera singers could shatter a wine glass with only their voice. Intense bass could cause nausea, headaches, collapsed lungs, or sudden arrhythmic death syndrome under the right circumstances.

Shandra's newest project was in a similar field. She'd discovered a frequency of ultrasonic sound that could damage the brain, rattling it inside the skull like a jalopy engine. The subject rapidly went insane as their neurons shook away their connections and the brain started to vibrate itself into warm tapioca.

It wasn't her favorite project, but she didn't get to decide what she worked on. There was only one problem. The lab was in the middle of a containment breach. A piece of dampening shield had fallen off the test chamber.

Shandra held her hands over her ears even though she knew it wouldn't help. The noise wasn't something she could hear. The frequency was too low for the human ear to detect. But she could feel it. It thumped and pulsed in her head, and it felt like her skull wanted to split open like a lizard egg.

She staggered toward the emergency shutoff switch, her senses battered and crumbling. Her thoughts didn't want to form properly. They felt warped and rubbery, like they'd been hammered together by a pair of drunks. She lurched forward, feeling her mind slipping as her thoughts danced around to the unnatural pulse like squirrels performing liturgical dance for a dark squirrel deity.

Nothing made sense anymore. She groped for the shutoff switch. She had to get that awful, throbbing beat out before her head exploded. She had to get it out, out, out! The original plan dissolved away in favor of something better.

Shandra grabbed the power drill and placed it to her temple.

THIRTY-TWO

LIGHTS OUT

Murphy sat in the dark with the other survivors. The power was out. It had been out for a couple of days now. Supposedly, the National Guard was working to get it back on, but Murphy didn't even know if those guys were still alive anymore. He kind of doubted it.

Those *things* were absolutely everywhere out there. He knew for sure that he wouldn't be alive if he was stuck outside with them. Right now, he couldn't see any out there in the moonlight, but he knew they were there. Given the opportunity, they'd tear him and everyone else in here apart.

Right now, the plan was to wait for morning and then assess whether or not they could make a break for it. The creatures weren't as active during the daylight hours. That didn't mean they weren't out there, though. He'd been in the traffic jam trying to get out of town, the National Guard directing traffic, and a whole bunch of them came out of the woods. They took the soldiers out and then starting attacking the cars. He wasn't sure how he made it out alive. Pure, dumb luck, mostly.

Everyone else in the little abandoned house had a similar story. Ernie had been a mechanic. Those things attacked, and he had to hop in the car he was working on and drive away. Made it about to the edge of town without a wheel before he had to abandon the vehicle and run. Mitch was a police officer. He still had his gun, but he was out of ammo. He kept checking his radio, but he couldn't pick anything up except static.

Murphy didn't know the lady's story. He'd found out her name was Susan, but she didn't talk much. She had a few bandages stuck on her arms and legs. Murphy knew that she'd been holed up in this farmhouse longer than anyone, but he didn't think she lived here.

Suddenly, half the lights in the house all snapped on at once. The smoke detectors beeped. The microwave clock started blinking.

"Get the lights," Murphy shouted. He ran to the nearest switch and slapped at it. He accidentally turned more lights on. Slapping them off, he found the correct switch on the far wall. They were lit up like a damn Christmas tree. The Guardsmen at the powerplant had the electricity back on, the idiots.

Murphy couldn't find the switch for the porch light. They'd successfully turned everything off indoors, but the outside light still glowed. Was the switch outside? They had to find it.

But it was too late.

One of the moths crashed against the side of the house, seeking out the light. It's eight-foot wingspan blocked out the windows. It bonked against the side of the house again, trying to get to the porch light. More giant, black-winged shapes descended from the sky as the walls started to buckle from repeated impacts.

THIRTY-THREE

BOB LARSON: PARANORMAL INVESTIGATOR

The white pickup truck looked like the sort of vehicle a freelance plumber or general contractor might use. There was a ladder strapped to the top and some equipment sitting in the bed. But for the company name printed on the side, no one would have paid the vehicle any mind. *Bob Larson: Paranormal Investigator.*

"Well, Miss. Here's what I found. You have some faulty plumbing. That can rattle or even make the sort of moaning and groaning noises you complained about. Heating isn't my specialty, but I noticed your vent filters are old, too. That can make some noise," Bob said.

The homeowner held her hand over her heart. "Oh, you don't know what this means to me, Mr. Larson. I kept hearing things in the middle of the night, and it would scare the bejeezus out of me. I didn't know what to tell my kids. I was dreading coming back here at night."

Bob smiled. "No need to thank me. It's just what I do. I'm not one of those charlatans that's going to tells you he has psychic powers and that you've got ghosts out the yin-yang. This sort of thing is almost always because of something simple going wrong in the structure itself."

"But what about the odor that came sometimes? I could swear that the whole place smelled like…" The woman glanced around as if spies were hanging out of the bushes, listening for juicy secrets. "*Death*," she finished.

"I mentioned that venting of yours. Most likely, you just have a mouse that died in there somewhere. If the heat comes on and cooks the little guy a bit…" Bob said.

"I'll go inside and get my checkbook. You have no idea how relieved I am. I kept going back and forth thinking that I was either going crazy and it was all in my head or that the place was haunted. Just knowing that it was real and something rational takes a load off my shoulders."

"Like I said. Just doing my job. I'm just going to pop in my truck and check on a work order while you go inside. See you in a minute."

Bob waited until the homeowner went back inside before sitting down behind the wheel. He rolled up his sleeve and plopped an ashtray down in the cupholder, feeling good. He pulled a pack of matches and something else out of his pocket before glancing back at the house.

Then, he looked down at the elaborate tattoo on his forearm and drew the pocketknife across it. Blood dribbled out and landed in the ashtray. The tattoo pulsed and throbbed with a life of its own. He bandaged the gash up and tossed a lit match into the bloody ashtray.

A gout of smoke and flame erupted from the ashtray. The smoke wafted out the open window, leaving behind a faint wisp. The little line of smoke danced up from the black, crusted layer of blood in the ashtray. The wisp shimmied and wavered, despite the lack of a breeze. From the right angle, the line of smoke could almost be mistaken for the silhouette of a face.

"Pretty standard," Bob said to the smoke. "The pipes are faulty. It sounds like they moan during the night sometimes. Occasional smell of death. If you can imitate that, she'll never even know you're there until it's too late."

The face seemed to nod before disappearing. Bob pulled his sleeve down over his tattoo as the homeowner came back outside. He got back out of his truck and smiled.

THIRTY-FOUR
HEIST

Calvin waved his sawn-off shotgun in the general direction of the bank employees. They lay on the floor, pale-faced and frightened.

"Everybody just needs to stay nice and calm. No need to be alarmed. We're just going to take what's ours, and then we'll be on our way. Got it? Hmm? Let me hear you say you got it."

A couple of the bank employees nodded. Some of them just lay there, completely frozen.

Calvin blasted the shotgun into the ceiling, sending plaster raining down on top of the people in front of him. They jumped or screamed or whimpered. The sound of the shotgun was deafening in the enclosed space.

He pulled his ski mask up so his mouth wasn't covered anymore. "Did I mumble? All together now. Do you get it?"

The employees all stammered through some version of what he wanted to hear. Good.

"Easy there, cowboy," Beth said. "Let's keep the masks on and the noise down to a dull roar. We don't need any heat coming our way too fast."

"Okay, Pookie Bear," Calvin said. But he still looked up at one of the security cameras and blew a raspberry before he lowered his mask the rest of the way. He wasn't worried about the camera footage. He was too keyed up to worry about anything right now.

Every inch of his body was covered up again. Mask. Sunglasses. Gloves. Padded shirt and pants. Not a single identifiable feature. The cameras wouldn't get anything useful.

He and Beth were at the top of their game. Bonnie and Clyde had nothing on this. Once Johnny finished tossing everything into their goody bags, they'd dive into the getaway car and be out of here before the cops knew anything had happened. Slick as shit through a goose.

Johnny emerged from the back of the bank with a bunch of plain paper shopping bags. "Divide your spoils, ladies and germs. Time's up. We need to boogie."

"You grabbed everything?" Calvin asked, gesturing toward the back with his shotgun.

"Everything worth grabbing," Johnny said. His words were a little muffled behind his own mask, but Calvin believed him. Johnny knew his stuff.

Calvin snatched up a bag, but he couldn't resist a quick glimpse inside. This was indeed the good stuff. They'd live like kings off of this. Everything was nicely labeled and stacked. Perfect.

Beth and Johnny hustled out of the front doors toward the waiting car. Calvin brought up the rear, keeping his shotgun ready. "Thanks for the memories. Toodles," he said, blowing a kiss at the shaken employees before piling into the rumbling car.

They sped away, and Calvin lifted up the lower half of his mask again. He kissed Beth on her masked cheek and then tore open the bag at his feet.

Then he lifted up one of the packets and sank his fangs into it. Cold blood gushed into his mouth. Type AB-negative, the rarest blood type in the United States. The good stuff.

"Hey, don't Bogart the goods," Beth said. Calvin nodded and handed the punctured blood packet to her so she could have a go.

He pulled his mask down over his face again before the sunlight could burn him any further. The blood bank disappeared in the distance behind them.

THIRTY-FIVE
RISE AGAIN

General Josiah Gorgas sighed as his office door banged open. As the Confederacy's chief of ordinance, he was a very busy man. When the war broke out, the South had only a scattering of foundries, most of which were unsuitable for arms productions. Acquiring guns required hiring blockade runners and privateers willing to scurry past the Union's ships. Finding the saltpeter needed to actually supply rebel troops with gunpowder was another herculean task that consumed a great deal of his time.

He'd turned Albert Whittaker away time and time again already, but the man refused to take no for an answer. When he'd heard that Whittaker had arrived, completely uninvited, at the military depot, Gorgas had ordered his secretary to stall the man until he could be tossed out. But Whittaker had found a way to fight his way past the secretary and enter the office.

"General Gorgas! We meet at last. I've been sending you letters, but I don't know if you've received them."

"I know who you are, Mr. Whittaker," Gorgas said, not bothering to look up from procurement sheets he was filling out.

"Good. Perfect, even! Then you must surely know of the revolutionary new system I'd like to provide our armies with," Whittaker said.

Gorgas looked up for the first time and rubbed his eyes. Whittaker was a small man who exuded energy. His eyes never seemed to stop moving, and his rocked back and forth from his toes to his heels, as if he would burst if he stopped moving.

"Mr. Whittaker, I will be frank. I do not have the time or patience for whatever brand of inanity you wish to present me with. Please leave."

"But, General. I am a patriot; I have a great deal to offer. I will not be dissuaded so easily. Allow me five minutes of your time, just five minutes, and if you are not convinced, I will never darken your door again. No letters. No visits. I shall return to private business for the duration of the war."

Gorgas sighed and stood up from his chair. Whittaker spoke so quickly, and he buzzed with so much twitchy enthusiasm, that it was exhausting just tolerating his presence. "Very well. I'll either be rid of you or find something useful. Either is acceptable."

Whittaker seemed as if he would positively blossom with joy. He gestured for Gorgas to follow him and the general reluctantly did so.

Stepping outside for the first time in hours, Gorgas blinked in the sunlight. He glanced around and immediately realized what Whittaker wanted to offer him.

The chained black men stood in the courtyard, their rotting flesh halfway through the process of sliding off their bones in the humid, Southern heat. Wires and electrodes poked out of their decaying flesh, snaking in and out of their bodies and wrapping from limb to limb. Their hollow, dead eyes stared straight ahead, but their mouths never stopped a slow, hungry chewing motion. Whittaker had dressed them all in a crude approximation of the butternut grey rebel uniform, though the cloth was stained with crusted blood and oozing bile.

"I can begin mass production immediately. With your blessing, of course," Whittaker said.

THIRTY-SIX
YOU NEVER CAN TELL

"Oh my goodness," Marjorie said.

Darrel's fork full of meatloaf stopped halfway to his mouth. He'd been married to Marjorie long enough to know that *oh my goodness* was code that she wanted to talk about something juicy. Right now, she was reading the paper on the couch while he polished off dinner.

She was the only person he knew who still read a physical newspaper. Even the old folks in the ground floor apartment either watched the news on their television or read it on a phone. He knew because they were half deaf and they listened to the tv far too loud. He could play along to the gameshow they watched after the news. But Marjorie liked the paper. She liked the tactile element, she always said.

"What is it?" Darrel said, knowing that she was just dying for an excuse to tell him.

"The police arrested Victor Morton from down the block. They found out he was selling human body parts on the black market, and they raided his medical center."

"Wait, really? We've been going to him for years." Darrel was flabbergasted.

"It says it right here," Marjorie said, poking a stubby finger at the paper. "Police raided the doctor's office and discovered a veritable charnel house in the basement, with parts from as many as six different bodies."

Darrel put his fork down and thought back to all the times he'd seen Victor. The man lived not far away. They often ran into each other walking their dogs or just grabbing milk from the store. They never talked personal details much, either when Darrel came in for serious business or when they ran into each other by chance. He tried to think if Victor had ever said anything odd. Given any indication. Tipped his hand at all. But there was nothing.

"Just goes to show, you never can tell about people," Darrel said.

"I know," Marjorie agreed. "All these years, and he never told us he was a doctor."

Darrel finished took another bite of meatloaf.

THIRTY-SEVEN
TAR PITS

Anthony Liu walked over the planks laid atop the tar. He and his team were excavating a particularly dense patch of fossil remains.

The tar pits were an extraordinary source of bones and other ancient material. The area naturally oozed asphalt and heavy tar. Left undisturbed, it would become covered in leaves and dust or even shallow water. Throughout history, animals would stumble into the black swamp, either by accident or pursued by predators, and become trapped in the sticky goo. They'd struggle before dying of exhaustion, starvation, or simply suffocating in the tar. Then, the odor of their rotting corpses would attract scavengers and meat eaters of every variety, which would become trapped themselves.

The most remarkable aspect of the tar pits, at least to a paleontologist like Anthony, was how well the tar preserved the bones and skeletons. Bacteria and fungus that would normally eat away at the remains couldn't survive in the oily muck, either. That meant that everything was preserved much better than if it had laid down and died anywhere else.

He had pulled mammoths, saber-toothed cats, dire wolves, and ground sloths out of the earth here. Each and every one was remarkable, as far as he was concerned.

It was just a matter of finding them. Sifting through the muck wasn't easy. If he and his team weren't careful, it would try to suck them down just like the mammoths. Everyone on the crew had lost boots. The pit had swallowed a few phones and rings, too.

Anthony never knew what he was going to find on any particular day. Whenever they found anything under the ooze, it needed to be hauled up and cleaned before they could determine what it was. Sometimes, it was a titanic set of bones. Other times, it was a bunch of branches and trash.

Yesterday, the team had found something strange. Anthony still wasn't sure what it was. The thing wasn't natural. It was big and round, almost like some sort of old bathysphere. It was the biggest piece of manmade debris they'd ever pulled out of the tar. Anthony knew it was made out of metal, but he didn't know much else about what it was. Now that they'd winched it all the way out, it was time to hose it off, load it on the truck, and, in all likelihood, haul it off to the dump.

Anthony stepped up to the giant, shimmering ball of goo and pulled his gloves on. He grabbed a hose and started spraying the odd contraption down. More and more dented and corroded metal revealed itself as Anthony scrubbed.

Suddenly, he found something new. A clear, glass panel. He turned the hose on the glass and wiped it clean. Clean enough to see through, anyway.

He recoiled as he realized what was inside. Bodies. At least three of them. They lay on the floor inside, dry and mummified. It looked like they'd been there since the pyramids were young. All three of the individuals looked like a beef jerky sculpture.

Anthony pressed closer to the glass again. What the hell had he just found? It had to be a crime scene. Or the site of some kind of accident. Or it was some sort of sick practical joke. He gazed inside, trying to make out more details.

The interior was covered in switches, levers, and buttons. He could see chrome and brass everywhere, and something that looked vaguely like a giant sextant.

And above it all was a banner that hung from one side of the strange bathysphere to the other. MAIDEN VOYAGE OF SIR GORDON FREEMANTLE'S TIME MACHINE.

THIRTY-EIGHT
SURVIVORS

The zombie apocalypse, perhaps unsurprisingly, hit Baltimore hard. Probably why the situation was appended with "apocalypse."

Most of the downtown burned up shortly after the military evacuated. Everyone else was left to fend for themselves as the dead poured through the streets.

Carol moved slowly down the alleyway, looking for food. She was one of the ones the army left behind. These days, people ate what they could. A few lucky holdouts had rooftop gardens or access to canned food stores. Most scrounged what they could, which meant creeping out into the streets with the dead.

Off in the distance, Carol heard a rapid series of gunshots, three in quick succession. She started in that direction. By the time she arrived, the place might be swarming with ghouls. Or there might be a spilled backpack full of tins of old dog food. Or both. Opportunity knocked.

Moving down the street, sticking to the overgrown shadows, she picked her way past the shell of a hotel. Carol never liked living in Baltimore. She moved here for a job about a month before everything went to hell. Aside from the burned-out ambulance wedged halfway in the hotel, this area didn't even look that different from before the Collapse. Cracked concrete and stained walls and street lights that didn't work.

The more things changed.

A couple of ghouls moved through the parking lot, also headed toward the gunshots, but they didn't see Carol. She moved through the remains of a picked-clean convenience store. There was no food inside, only mold and the scattered remains of a skeleton.

Carol moved a little awkwardly. She had a heavy pack on her back, full of the various odds and ends needed to survive the city. It was heavy, but she never went anywhere without it.

Suddenly, the convenience store's rear door slammed open and a boy, barely old enough to shave, threw himself inside. He wheeled around and pushed the door shut again in the face of three zombies. He had a pistol in one shaking hand and a couple bags of expired junk food in the other.

Food! Sweet, precious food. It was the single most valuable commodity in this godforsaken city.

The boy turned around as Carol lurched forward, her cold, dead hands clamping down on his shoulders. He had just enough time to scream before her teeth clamped down on his throat.

THIRTY-NINE
RING

"Scans are coming back now," Hoffman said. "Ooh."

"Ooh?" Elle said. "Is that a good 'ooh' or a bad 'ooh?'"

"Real good. The planet's rings are rich in metal and mineral lodes. It's quite a mixture, actually. I've got everything from iron to iridium coming up on screen."

"Let's take 'er in and get to harvesting, then," Elle said, tapping commands into the mining vessel's computer.

Finding the planet in the first place had been a surprise. It wasn't on their survey charts. Then again, it wasn't the first time the survey teams had missed something. On the very outer edges of these systems, some of the planets had irregular orbits, making big, egg-shaped loops around their respective stars. The last time the company sent a survey crew through this corner of the galaxy was almost twenty standard Earth years ago.

Finding the ringed planet was a lucky break, though. If they could mine what they needed directly from space instead of landing on the planet, they'd save a lot of money on fuel. That meant a bigger commission.

The ring itself, while beautiful, was just debris. It was probably the result of a big meteor grazing the edge of the planet and spraying molten rock and metal into orbit, where it stabilized around the planet. Maybe one day, it would coalesce into a moon.

Or it would have, if Elle and Hoffman hadn't stumbled on it.

"Sending out a probe. Let's sample the goods," Hoffman said. He clacked at his controls, and a drone buzzed away from their vessel.

Finally, their probe returned to them. Elle and Hoffman were waiting for it by the main viewing platform when it did.

"Time to crack this baby open," Elle said, punching in a keycode and activating the decontamination process. A moment later, the contents spilled out.

"The hell?" Hoffman said.

The probe had coughed out a bunch of metal, as expected. But most of it was pulverized, processed metal. There were pieces of unidentifiable machinery, all crushed and smashed, but clearly not natural.

"These look likes parts of spacecraft," Elle said.

"Yeah, but blasted apart. I don't even think all of this is from human spacecraft. And this...I think this is bone," Hoffman said.

It was then that the planet below opened a cavernous mouth and started moving toward them. Elle raced back toward the craft's propulsion controls, but she was too late.

The debris field grew.

FORTY
SWAT

Heather Klein held the bullhorn in her hand as she watched the house. The red and blue lights from a dozen police cars, including the huge SWAT command truck, filled the night. One of the officers had delivered a telephone at the house's doorstep over two hours ago. Shortly thereafter, an arm had snaked out the door and grabbed it.

Communications had broken down with the hostage taker, though. He wasn't talking to them over the phone anymore. Even with her hostage negotiation training, Heather couldn't get the man to respond. She'd spent the last half hour talking into the bullhorn, but she hadn't gotten any results. Not so much as a peep.

That wasn't a good sign.

There hadn't been any gunshots or obvious signs of trouble from inside the home. But that wasn't necessarily a good thing. They didn't have any idea what was going on in there. They needed eyes and ears. Or at the very least, the needed the hostage taker focused on talking to Heather rather than working himself into a fidgety, twitchy lather. From the outside, the house in the sleepy little neighborhood looked calm and peaceful. Inside, it was a pressure cooker.

"I don't like this," Chief Mendel said.

"I'm trying everything I can," Heather said.

"Oh, I don't doubt that," the Chief said. "But we're not getting through to this guy. You have five more minutes. Then, I'm sending in SWAT."

Despite the coolness of the night, sweat stood out on Heather's forehead. The moon hung low and pregnant overhead, illuminating the whole scene.

She didn't want it to come down to the SWAT unit. If they went barging through the door, there almost certainly would be gunfire. There'd be blood and shouting. As effective as the unit was, they couldn't guarantee the safety of the hostages. Heather wanted a peaceful resolution, if there was one to be had.

She picked up the bullhorn again and starting talking. Her training kicked in. But training could only carry her so far. This was the real deal, and real lives were at stake.

Chief Mendel had wandered over to the SWAT truck, nodding to a couple of the specialists waiting nearby. Heather kept talking into the bullhorn, but her attention was on Mendel. There was no response from the house. The curtains didn't even flutter. The madman inside wasn't paying attention to her.

The specialists started unloading heavy steel cages from the truck. Heather caught a glimpse of a pair of reflective eyes inside the cage, feral and hungry. Once those cages opened, the Special Werewolf Assault Team would be free, and then it would be all over.

FORTY-ONE
UPON NIGHT'S LEATHERY WINGS

Murphy scrambled through the overgrown woods. His watch had stopped working, and he hadn't realized until it was too late. He'd spent all afternoon scrounging for supplies, totally unaware that the safety of daylight was slipping away from him.

He'd been forced to abandon the few items he'd found in favor of running for his life. He had to get back to his shelter before darkness fell. Hopefully, no one would steal his salvage before he could get to it again.

That was pretty unlikely. There weren't many people left alive in the military exclusion zone. The other survivors mostly stuck closer to the hills, where the thickness of the trees offered more cover. Murphy hadn't seen another human being in over forty days.

In theory, he could try to slip through the forest and find his way to an area that wasn't affected. He could try, but there was a good chance he'd be shot in the attempt. The damn giant moths weren't the only thing to worry about.

As if the caterpillars and the moths weren't bad enough, they'd brought disease with them. It rotted people from the inside out, like some sort of Dutch elm disease. A few people were immune to it, Murphy included. That didn't mean they couldn't be carriers, though. He knew for a fact that some of the containment teams had a name for him. Typhoid Murphy. He'd never leave this town or valley alive, if the government had anything to say about it.

It had always been important to get to safety before dark. He'd survived in part by keeping a strict schedule every day. That was more important than ever now that the military had developed a counter-weapon of sorts against the bugs.

He crashed through the trees, heedless of the cuts and scratches the branches gave him. He could bandage himself up later, but only if he survived. The government's new weapon would come online as soon as dusk fell, about the same time the bugs became most active.

The sun had already plunged to the very edge of the horizon. Something buzzed over the tree line, its translucent wings thrumming like a buzzsaw. The bugs were starting to come out.

Murphy burst into a clearing and instantly realized his mistake. He was out under the open sky. A moth the size of a small helicopter swept by overhead.

But that wasn't his biggest problem. The government countermeasures didn't discriminate. Years of research and development had been invested making the system deadly, not selective.

Another shadow swept by overhead as the last sliver of sunlight dipped below the horizon. Murphy looked up. The gigantic, government-bred bat dove out of the sky, its claws extended to scoop him up.

FORTY-TWO

USS ARMSTRONG

Vance Lockwood sat in the command chair, updating his captain's log. The *USS Armstrong*, pride of the fleet, had excelled in its test runs, and now it was cruising like a dream. The massive exploration vessel could probe deeper into space than any previous ship built by the Federated Planets. Its warp drive could catapult it from system to system in a matter of hours rather than days.

Captain Lockwood and his intrepid crew had already seen planets that no human eyes had ever beheld before. Their instruments had collected data that astronomers had been thirsting after for generations. He was most excited about the milestone they were about to hit, though.

In a matter of minutes, they'd emerge out of warp into a system that marked the halfway point across the galaxy. They weren't shooting directly into the galactic core, of course. The *Armstrong* was an amazing ship, but it would be torn apart by the blackholes and dense star factories present there. His navigating would skirt them around the far side, giving them a glimpse at the opposite side of the Milky Way. It made him feel like one of the old Earth explorers, pushing on toward a mysterious horizon.

The *Armstrong* lurched and the lights dimmed for a second as they entered the new system's heliosphere. Lockwood sat up in his command chair. He'd prepared a little speech to mark the momentous occasion. The other side of the galaxy. Truly a wonder.

"Sir, I'm detecting an errant signal," Executive Officer Gupta said.

"From one of the planets?" Lockwood asked. The *Armstrong* was yet to meet any new civilizations among the stars. If they discovered a planet with a society that had invented the radio, it would be another feather in his hat, and they'd take reams of documentation from afar.

"No, sir. It's spaceborne. The signals look like…ours."

"What?" Lockwood asked. Then, the command console lit up. A priority message. On their encrypted wavelength.

The message came through on the viewscreen automatically. Lockwood saw the bridge of a ship very much like the *Armstrong*. The viewscreen showed a number of people sitting around the bridge. One of them looked a lot like Executive Officer Gupta. *A lot* like Gupta. And the man in the command seat was the spitting image of Lockwood.

"Get engineering on the line. We've got some sort of malfunction," Lockwood and the man onscreen said at exactly the same time. "Odd," they both muttered, scratching their head in sync. Lockwood looked at the screen and used it to straighten his hair a little, like a mirror.

There was obviously a fault somewhere. A camera had turned on aboard the bridge and then the ship had flagged a call to itself. Annoying. And potentially dangerous in a combat situation.

"Engineering says they have nothing on their end." Gupta tapped at his command console. The Gupta on screen did the same. "Hold on we're getting a visual now."

The screen split to show a view of space. It zoomed in to show a ship. It showed the *Armstrong*. What the hell? They didn't have exterior probes that could get a shot like that. Even if the system had confused its feeds again, there was no way the ship could take a live picture of itself like that.

And as Lockwood looked closer, he saw that the ship on the screen wasn't named the *Armstrong*. The other ship had its own name on the side of the hull. The *USS Aldrin*.

"I'm getting some weird readings, Captain," Gupta said. A bevy of red lights blinked on his console.

"I don't like this. Get us out of this system," Lockwood said.

But the Lockwood on screen didn't say that.

"I don't like this. Fire the torpedoes."

FORTY-THREE

PRONUNCIATION

Sharon checked her phone while the kids scribbled away on their worksheets. For once, they were fairly focused, and none of them seemed to need help. There were a dozen different things she *should* be doing, but she needed a couple of minutes of personal time. Maybe she wasn't supposed to be checking social media during school hours, but this classroom was basically her personal fiefdom. Sharon Kowalski, supreme dictator for life of room B-12.

After a moment of scrolling, she kind of wished that she hadn't checked her phone after all. A bunch of her friends from the university teaching program were already out on summer break. There were vacation pictures at the beach, posts about hobbies and family time, and all manner of things she couldn't do yet. Gone were the countdowns until the end of the year and the flustered mini-screeds of new teachers adjusting to the reality of shepherding a bunch of children through the education system. She even missed Carrie's obnoxiously chipper posts about her always oh-so-perfect classroom.

But that was part of the price of working at a small religious school instead of the in the public school system. The board was under no obligation to follow the same schedule as public school, and that meant that Sharon's summer break started later than anyone else's.

It wasn't all bad, though. Everyone would get to be jealous of her when they were back in the classroom, and she still had a few more weeks of summer break. Until then, every trip to social media was an inadvertent torture session. The number of days on her calendar that needed to be crossed off never seemed to get smaller.

They were rapidly approaching the end of everything, though. The kids had a few more tests to get through, all of them based on the school's special curriculum. Right now, their language lessons were going remarkably well, for once.

Sharon turned her phone off and tried to look like she was doing something important as one of the students got out of his chair and came up to her desk.

He pointed at a phrase on his worksheet with a colored pencil. "How do you pronounce this?"

Sharon sighed. She liked that the school still had traditional language requirements in its religious curriculum, but it was annoying to repeat certain things over and over again.

"Ph'nglui mglw'nafh Cthulhu R'lyeh wgah'nagl fhtagn," she said, carefully enunciating everything.

Yes, soon she wouldn't be so jealous of those beach pictures and family fun posts. Soon.

FORTY-FOUR
MIRROR, MIRROR

Phaedra, real name Thelma Elizabeth Fischer, stared into the mirror. The house was dark. Her parents were still out for the night. The only illumination in the bathroom was a single, pumpkin-scented candle, the only candle Phaedra could find.

Her hair was died jet black, the color of stygian midnight. Except where the roots had grown out to reveal a bit of dark blond. Her thick, white makeup made her face a ghastly shade of pale white, like a freshly buried victim of consumption. Except for a few spots where her acne came through in angry red blotches. Her eye shadow was ringed in dark shadows, giving her eyes the appearance of glittering out from a skull. Except where it had smudged. Her black, frilled clothes looked like something a Victorian lady might wear to a friend's funeral. Except they were from a shop at the run-down mall at the edge of town.

Tenth grade was hard, and pretty much everything sucked. Frankly, Phaedra was miserable. The other students at her school didn't understand her. The ones who didn't do their best to ignore her were usually cruel and stupid. Her parents didn't understand her, and her brother's sole mission in life was to torment her.

There was only one thing she could think to do.

"Bloody Mary," she said into the mirror.

Maybe it was just in her imagination, but a chill fell over everything. The house was quiet before, but it descended into total silence now.

"Bloody Mary," Phaedra said again. It was like everything outside the house fell away. Everything beyond the bathroom door was frozen in time. The darkness pressed against the door, heavy and hungry.

"Bloody Mary."

The candle flickered. Guttered. Nearly went out. Then, it returned, but lower and darker than before. Phaedra could barely even see her own face in the mirror anymore. She was simply a pale smudge in the blackness.

Then, a second smudge appeared, gray and waifish. There were streaks of red, dripping and oozing down into the darkness. Slowly, the smudge resolved into a face. The skin was in the process of sloughing off the skull like a melted rubber mask. Damp, stringy hair clung all around the pale face, dripping with red. Eyes like potholes on hell's highway stared directly into Phaedra's.

"Hi, Mary. My parents won't be back until tomorrow. Ready for the sleepover?"

The figure nodded, pulling itself through the mirror frame on a set of rickety, skeletal claws.

FORTY-FIVE
GONE FISHING

Wilson pulled up near the dock. Not at the dock. Too many people. Not good conditions. Better to be off by himself for this.

He finally found the perfect spot and parked his ship, where the water was calm. The fog had rolled in, blocking the sun and keeping things nice and cool. He couldn't stand when it was hot, and the light reflected off the water and blinded him. This was how fishing was meant to be done, a solitary, meditative experience. Perhaps a couple of drinks. Just a quiet day by the sea on his rig.

Carefully baiting his hook, Wilson dropped his line near some rocks close to shore. Now the waiting began.

A few people walked up and down the beach, leading dogs or children. A group of teenagers pulled up at one point but quickly moved on, evidently dissatisfied with the cloudy sky. Another fisherman briefly stopped but evidently decided he wanted more company and quickly picked up and moved to the dock with everyone else. Fine with Wilson.

He was hoping to bring a big, tasty prize back home with him today. Less likely, he could reel in something interesting that he might want to stick over his mantle. He'd always had good luck at this spot, and he was pretty sure that it was because he avoided the dock.

Cracking open the first drink of the day, he sat back and waited, watching. Nothing happened for a good, long while. He reeled his line back in and cast it in a different spot. By the time he was done with the first can, he cast to a third location.

Suddenly, the line twitched. It twitched again. He put down the second can and grabbed the pole. The line gave a bigger twitch, and Wilson jerked the line back. Suddenly the line didn't just twitch. It tried to yank out of his hands. It strained and pulled as something thrashed on the end of the hook.

Wilson worked the reel, hauling his prize up from below. He gritted his teeth, putting more effort into it. Finally, his line came up even with the craft, and he hauled it aboard.

The man was screaming, the big, metal hook impaled through his hand. Blood jetted out where the metal barb had punched through his palm.

Wilson pulled the hundred dollar bill off the hook first and then yanked the man's hand off second. He grabbed his captive and tossed him in the cooler. Wiping the bloody stain off the money, he reattached it to the hook and lowered the line again.

If he got some more bites, he'd stay parked here. If things dried up or the Earthling military showed up, he'd take the flying saucer to the next watering hole.

FORTY-SIX

CAVIAR

"It all sounds so good," Juanita said, eyeing the menu.

"Honestly, I'm struggling to decide what to get next, and it's all so…" Steve held his hand up, fingers clasped together as he groped for just the right word.

"Avant-garde?" Juanita tried.

"Yes, but it's more than that. They're just so inventive. I've never been anywhere that offers such a range of options. It's truly high-end, experimental dining. They seem to have a unique twist on everything, not just the Southwestern food."

The waiter came up to the food critics. Steve and Juanita clammed up. They'd already plowed through a pair of appetizers. They didn't want word to spread back to the kitchen that there'd be an article about this place in the paper tomorrow. That might lead to additional extravagances, and they both knew they wanted the authentic experience.

"Have you both decided what you'd like for the main course?"

"I'm intrigued by the special," Juanita said.

"Ah, yes, the desert caviar."

"What exactly makes it 'desert' caviar?"

"Well, as you no doubt know, caviar is salt-cured roe from fish. Fish eggs, essentially. The traditional dish uses eggs from sturgeon, though trout or carp may be used in some countries."

"Of course," Steve said.

"We use a non-traditional source, served alongside our rustic masa tortilla nachos and a meat pâté."

"I think we'll have an order of that for the table," Steve said.

"Excellent choice, sir," the waiter said, jotting the order down on his notepad. He turned around and started back toward the kitchen.

"I can't wait to try it," Juanita whispered to Steve.

The waiter pushed his way through the swinging double doors and shut them as quickly as possible. He turned around to the chef, who was wielding an oversized mallet like a cudgel.

"I need more tarantula eggs for the desert caviar," the waiter said.

"Okay, let me get the pâté ready," the chef said before bringing the mallet down on another spider.

FORTY-SEVEN

FOG

Gail watched the fog roll in over the northern end of town, enveloping the highway. The mist had come in overnight, creeping toward the old lighthouse. She sat on her porch, watching the ocean and town from atop the hill her house was situated on.

It was a strange fog, always sticking low to the ground. Even as the day wore on, the sun couldn't seem to burn it off. Whenever a breeze kicked up, it would ripple but refuse to blow away.

She'd planned to spend most of the day working on the quilt she'd been making, but, as happened quite often, watching the outside world had distracted her. Today, it wasn't just the beauty of the coastline that had sent her wool gathering, though.

The old lighthouse was on fire. Smoke belched out of the mostly gutted structure, but flames continued to crawl across the blackened beams and had found a couple of cars in the parking lot, turning them to angry husks. The fog turned the flames weirdly fuzzy from a distance, like she was looking at everything through cotton candy.

It was a horrible shame to lose a historic structure like that. Gail would miss the lighthouse spire jutting up over the town, protecting the bay.

What she didn't understand was why the fire department hadn't saved the lighthouse. The town's sole firetruck sat in the lighthouse parking lot. From up here, she could see the big, red vehicle's flashing lights. She couldn't see the fire crew, but as far as she could tell, they hadn't done anything to put the flames out. They'd simply let them gutter low, now that there was nothing left.

She had an old pair of Herb's binoculars somewhere from when he took up birdwatching for a week. Scrounging around the attic, Gail finally found them in a box and brought them back to her porch.

By the time she made it back down, the fog had crept over more of the town, and another bank of mist had enveloped the highway to the south, blocking the town off. A car sped out of town, going far too fast for the weather, and plowed through the mist. She scowled to see such unsafe driving. Gail watched its headlights disappear completely, swallowed whole by the mist. An ember of unease kindled to life in Gail's chest.

She put the binoculars to her eyes. She could see the firefighters down by the lighthouse in their yellow reflective gear, but something was wrong. They were suspended in the fog, like marionettes hung up by a careless puppeteer. None of them were moving; they simply floated in the air, like some sort of magician's trick.

The fog billowed closer, even as she watched, moving to the base of her hill in awful slow motion, swallowing more of the town in the process. The wind wasn't driving it. It wasn't coming off the ocean. It moved with a will of its own. It was a slow but sinister process, easing up on her hilltop a few feet at a time like a cautious predator. Gail bit her lip, hoping the low-hanging fog would gather around the base of her hill but not climb it.

No such luck. The fog started to move upward, creeping ever closer. Gail thought about hopping in her truck and driving away, but she thought about those car headlights simply vanishing. She thought about the firefighters, suspended and unmoving in the mist. She didn't want to set foot in the fog, if she didn't have to.

Then, Gail received a visitor, and she realized what was happening. Then another visitor. And another. The spiders made their way up the hill, gathering around her house, swarming past it until the ground was black with bristly little bodies. The small spiders came first, but then bigger and bigger variations came, creeping up the porch, covering the house.

And they built their webs as they went. The mist approaching wasn't a mist at all. It was a blanket of webbing.

FORTY-EIGHT

REWARD

The battered leaflet was nailed to the telephone pole in front of Nicole's house. It wasn't the only flier pinned there. There were advertisements for guitar lessons and some kid's summer lawn service and a garage sale that ended over a month ago. But this flier was different.

It was a lost pet poster. The words were written in marker. Not permanent marker. Colorful children's markers. Nicole moved down her walkway and looked at the flier more closely.

LOST

Our pet, Mr. Tinkles, is missing. Please help us find him. Mr. Tinkles is grey with darker markings. He is afraid of most strangers and will not come if called. We love him very much, and there is a reward for his return.

Then, the poster listed a phone number.

There wasn't a picture of the lost animal. Instead, the kids who made the flier had drawn their pet. They were not particularly good artists. The animal could have been a cat or a dog or a gazelle. Nicole really couldn't tell much about it beyond the fact that it had four legs, a tail, and a face.

She started to walk back to her car so she could go to work when a helicopter flew low overhead. It was a big, dark helicopter, not one of the little things the local news teams sent out whenever traffic was bad or there was a car chase on the freeway. Two more helicopters buzzed past, still surprisingly low. Then, a lone news chopper went chasing after them.

One of the big, fat helicopters veered off and hovered some distance away, closer to the middle of her neighborhood. A sound system crackled to life.

"Citizens, stay indoors. This is an emergency situation. Do not, I repeat, do not enter the downtown area. Stay indoors until you are given the all clear." Then, the helicopter swerved away to follow its brothers.

Nicole watched it go for a minute. A few of her neighbors came out on the street to see what the commotion was about. The hell was this all about?

Mrs. Renfro from down the block came running down the street, still in her robe. "It's on the news! It's on the news!"

Nicole decided to head back inside. She didn't know what was going on, but it didn't sound good. Those helicopters looked like they belonged to the military. Maybe there'd been an accident. Toxic chemicals from a derailed train. A nuclear meltdown. Y2K, a few decades late and a dollar short.

She went inside and flipped on the news. She caught the local anchor mid-sentence.

"…scenes of destruction unlike anything I've ever seen before. There are at least two fires burning from ruptured gas lines, and significant damage to all the nearby buildings. It's a very clear path of destruction. Hold on. I'm being told that the News 6 chopper is in position. We should be getting fresh footage now."

The screen cut away to a scene of flattened buildings and billowing dust. Nicole didn't know what she was looking at until some of the dust parted.

There was a creature, a massive creature. It was the size of a small cruise ship, and it was trundling through downtown, flattening everything in its path. The hideous, four-legged beast plowed its way through a police barricade, tossing cars aside like toys. The creature had a gray hide, gray with darker markings.

FORTY-NINE

XIII

Jennifer woke up on the gurney. She looked around. She was in an elevator. A couple members of the hotel staff stood next to the gurney, not really paying attention to her. The elevator doors closed, and one of the workers pushed a button. Clanking and grinding, the old elevator began to descend.

What the hell? How did she get here? Her throat was parched to the point of pain. She tried to swallow, but her mouth was dry. Her head ached like someone was marching around in there, pounding on a drum. Her stomach quivered and lurched in a way that had nothing to do with the elevator's movement.

Jennifer tried to move her arm, but it wouldn't cooperate. She could nudge it around and bit, but it was like trying to push a dead rat uphill with a stick. Summoning her strength, she tried to sit up, but that rocket failed on liftoff. Her head made it maybe a couple of centimeters off the pillow before it sank back down.

Frustration burned in her veins. This was the Intercontinental, the best hotel in the state. Her uncle owned the skyscraper hotel, and effectively all the people in it. He'd renovated the old art deco building into something valuable again. There was something wrong, very obviously wrong, and neither of the workers seemed the least bit interested in offering her any help. They weren't even paying attention to her.

She tried to figure out what happened. Her brain didn't want to focus, though. She remembered a party. A party in the penthouse. She had told her uncle that it was a networking meeting, which wasn't entirely wrong. There were a lot of influential people in attendance. A couple of B-list movie stars. Some real estate people with connections. A lone Russian billionaire.

And pills. Lots of pills. Jennifer remembered taking some of the yellow ones, and she didn't remember much of anything after that.

Ah, balls. She must have passed out. The hotel staff had been called, and they were dragging her off to some facility somewhere.

At least they were being discrete about it, using the freight elevator instead of allowing paramedics to haul her out in front of the paparazzi. But her uncle would still hear about the whole thing, and then she'd be in the dog house.

Mustering up a little bit of strength again, she twisted her head around to look at the staff. Then, she noticed something. The button lit up on the elevator's control panel.

The thirteenth floor.

But she knew for a fact that the hotel didn't have a thirteenth floor. Not a formal one, anyway. Like a lot of old buildings, the floors jumped from the twelfth to the fourteenth. It kept the more superstitious guests happy.

She tried to ask the staff what was going on, but she only managed to make a muffled gargling noise. One of the workers noticed and looked down at her.

"Well, look who's decided to join us again. How are you feeling?"

"Bad." Jennifer managed to choke the word out. It popped free of her throat like a chicken bone Heimliched across the dining room. After a second of recuperation, she managed to shove a few more words out of her mouth. "Thirteenth floor?"

"It's kind of a staff area. Nobody else sees it," the other employee said. "We need to get you fitted for one of these snazzy, red jackets. You'll be running room service duty to start off."

"My uncle owns this place. I don't work here," Jennifer said.

"You do now," the first employee said. He lifted his arm up and pulled his own jacket sleeve down a little. There were cut marks down the length of his wrist, old but unhealed. Then she saw the bullet hole through the side of the other employee's head. Now that she had a better look at him, he looked a lot like the guy who had committed suicide in one of the rooms a couple of years ago.

She suddenly realized that she hadn't just passed out from the pills.

FIFTY

UPSTREAM

"If this is a joke, it's not a funny one," the prosecutor said.

"I don't joke about work," the medical examiner responded, tying a rubberized smock around her waist. "I'll show you."

"But a *mermaid*?" The prosecutor followed the medical examiner through the heavy double doors.

The medical examiner yanked the sheet off the table and revealed the form below. Rot hadn't set in yet, but the woman's hair was wet, and her body was swollen and bloated with gas.

The prosecutor had seen worse, especially from corpses pulled out of the river. What he'd never seen before was a body that tapered into a scaly fishtail instead of legs. Even though the woman's upper body looked basically human, her face was all wrong. Her mouth was contorted into a hideous death grimace, revealing a set of grisly needle teeth.

"What the...? This has to be fake. It's rubber or something."

"Nope. Very real. I've done some tests. Real blood. Real hair. Could be sewn together out of body parts, but I can't find any seam lines," the medical examiner said.

"Cripes. If it's made from a real body, that's either murder or desecration of a corpse."

"That's why I called you. Only one way to find out. I need to do an autopsy." The medical examiner wheeled over a set of steel tools, and the prosecutor looked away.

"How long has she been dead? There's not much rot, but she's bloated up." The prosecutor forced his eyes back to the corpse.

"Can't say yet. That's unusual, though."

"Not much about this is the usual."

"Everything seems organic so far," the medical examiner said, cutting further. "No signs of tampering. This looks like the genuine article. And this is saltwater in this bladder here."

"But you said she was found in the river."

"Right. She must have swum upstream."

"Like a salmon."

"Like a salmon," the medical examiner agreed.

"If she is a…mermaid and not some murder victim, I don't know that I can do anything about this," the prosecutor said. "You need zoologists, not lawyers."

"Hold on a second, I've found a mass." The medical examiner had her hand in the creature's swollen belly.

Then, the medical examiner screamed. She ripped her arm out of the corpse, and the district attorney saw something clutched in her gloved hand.

No, the hand wasn't holding the thing. It was holding onto the medical examiner's hand, sinking its tiny needle teeth through the gloves and tearing at flesh and tendons.

Then, the whole body began to thrash and twitch as dozens of small, nightmarish forms erupted out of it and began flopping onto the floor, going for the medical examiner's feet and crawling toward the prosecutor.

Suddenly, he understood. The mermaid had come upstream like a salmon. But salmon came upriver to die. And spawn. She wasn't swollen from rot and decay. She was pregnant.

Then, the wave of ravenous baby mermaids was upon him.

You're still here. I hope you're proud of yourself. That last time really freaked me out. I don't think it's just you who's the problem. Sure, you're the one dragging people up to the chopping block, but you're not the one with the axe.

FIFTY-ONE
FLINT

Dr. Camilla Bramwell examined the mummified figure laying on the cave floor. She'd never seen anything quite like this fine specimen. It predated modern man; that much was obvious. Without further examination of the body, it was impossible to say exactly what she was looking at. Maybe *Homo erectus*. Maybe *Homo habilis*. Maybe something else entirely.

It was a truly remarkable find. The cold, still air inside the cavern had apparently preserved the dead hominid's body, almost like a giant refrigerator. Given that the cave system was so close to the city, it was doubly remarkable that the site hadn't been previously disturbed. Visions of grant funding and publishable papers danced in her head.

Ancient hominids were known exclusively from scattered bones and fragmented tools. After hundreds of thousands of years, humanity's ancestors had been scavenged by hungry animals or decayed into dust. It was rare to find a particularly intact skeleton. To find something as well-preserved as a genuine mummy was absolutely unheard of.

She eyed the decrepit body. The ancient man had obviously been left here in a ritualistic manner, a sort of simple burial. He was sitting up, his back to the stone wall. He still clutched a flint hand axe in one gnarled hand. The axe didn't have a handle. It was simply a sharp wedge of rock. In all likelihood, it had been a prized possession buried with its owner, but Camilla didn't want to jump to any conclusions.

The whole cave was evidently one, big burial site. There were a large number of hominid bones scattered around the cave, most of them cracked and broken and yellowed with age. Camilla was curious about those, too. Even if they weren't as spectacular to study, they provided an interesting puzzle, too.

The cavern was positively littered with bones. But why weren't they as well preserved as the mummified man? Nearly all the bones in the cave looked like they'd been set upon by animals.

They were chewed and snapped open, the marrow sucked out. Why would animals devour most of the corpses and leave one alone?

Camilla squatted down next to one dismembered skeleton and examined it more closely. The ancient hominid's skull was shattered, as if dashed against the rock floor. She eyed the bones, mentally piecing them together.

The skull didn't look like a *Homo erectus* or a *Homo habilis* specimen. It didn't have the sloped, beetle-browed skull of the typical ancestral hominids. And the bones hadn't just been chewed, though they were gnawed and covered with numerous bite marks. They'd been scraped clean. There were grooves where a tool of some sort had rasped over the bone, shearing the flesh loose.

And there was something else among the bones. A little piece of metal. No, plastic. Camilla stared at the object. She didn't dare move anything, lest she disturb the site and ruin the *in situ* bones. She shone her light closer, and she realized what she was looking at.

It was a pair of glasses. Modern, cheap glasses. They'd been smashed and mangled until they were little more than shards. And there! A single, brass cufflink.

Camilla stood up. Something was wrong here. These bones hadn't been here long. Years, maybe. But not hundreds of thousands of them.

Now that she was looking closer, she saw more items that didn't belong. And a lot of the scattered bones were new, too new. It looked almost like…. It looked like a procession of people had wandered into the cave, found the mummy, and then unexpectedly perish, evidently with a great deal of violence.

She heard something moving in the darkness with her. It was a leathery, creaking noise, like an old saddle on the verge of falling apart. Then, the flint axe blade crashed down on top of her head.

I think whoever is organizing these stories is forcing the issue. The writer, if you will. A week ago, I never would have believed that someone was, well, writing my life. Frankly, I don't think most of my life has been written. I'm my own man. Nobody pulls George's strings. But the end? Yeah, I think that's been written. And when you read it, it's going to come down on me like an avalanche.

FIFTY-TWO

CUTTHROAT COMPETITION

Jeb chainsawed another camp counselor in half. He paused for a moment and popped his knuckles. His hands were covered in old burn marks and healed cuts.

It was hard being an independent slasher these days. The big slasher conglomerates could hire a couple of dozen murderers, each one more inbred and blood-simple than the last, and clear out one of these big summer camps in a few hours.

But they didn't do it with the personal touches that Jeb could offer. It was the little things. The pyramid of human hands left at the cabins for the police to find. The severed heads hollowed out like jack-o-lanterns. Toying with the final counselor for nearly an entire night before the cat and mouse game came to its inevitable conclusion. Those sorts of services just weren't available from the big slasher chains.

Jeb's father had been a killer, and Jeb had taken up the mantle. Still, it was hard for the little mom and pop operations like his to compete these days. A lot of the old places had shut down, the killers either arrested or defeated by precocious teenagers. It was enough to make Jeb sick sometimes to see killers his dad had teamed up with, men and women and things who should have been enjoying their golden years, locked up and left to rot.

He'd been forced to embrace innovation in order to survive. He loved the classic traditions, including the machetes and axes, but he needed to put food on the table, too. Maybe he was just getting old, but the job didn't have the same *je ne sais quoi* now that he had to adapt to the twenty-first century and keep up with the big guys. Dismembering guidance counselors one at a time would never be boring exactly, but he did harbor a certain yearning for the halcyon days when an aggrieved killer could do his job with little more than a pointy stick.

Cracking his neck, Jeb put the headset back on. The sounds of screams and pleas for mercy surrounded him again, cheap and tinny through the microphone. He took the control stick, and watched the remote-control drone's flightpath through the woods on his screen. The chainsaw mounted on the drone revved, and someone screamed so loud he could hear it from his work station at the dilapidated cabin.

Jeb sighed. It just wasn't the same.

Look, this has all gone to crap. I'm not trying to ruin everything for you. I'm trying to save myself. Everyone else if I can, too. But you have to work with me. You can't let us die like this.

FIFTY-THREE
IDOL HANDS

Dr. Ian Garrity emerged from the cave and stuffed the golden idol into his pack. He'd found it. After years of searching, he'd found it. The solid gold idol was his.

It was an incredible find. Archeologists had spent years searching for the ancient temple and the treasures it contained. Garrity actually found it, though. He'd discovered a scroll, tucked so far back in the ancient library that it had probably been untouched for hundreds of years.

The scroll didn't translate well into any living language, but in so many words, they'd warned that the idol was well-protected. That might have been true a thousand years ago, when extinct empires still fought wars over these lands, but there were no guards or warrior-priests to keep infidels from the inner sanctum now. The "Chamber of a Thousand Daggers" held no danger in the modern era.

Researchers could spend years studying the idol. A hundred grad students could write about its cultural significance in this little-understood corner of the world.

They could. But they wouldn't. This baby was going straight on the black market. Its golden body and jewel-encrusted eyes would serve as the center piece of some billionaire's private museum, and Garrity's bank account would go from empty to full.

The little pot-bellied humanoid figure, holding its little golden knives, would look beautiful under a glass case somewhere. The idol was kind of ugly, actually. It looked like a gilded goblin, and the garish figure would clash with any sort of tasteful home décor.

He felt the weight of the idol in his pack as he walked down the well-concealed path, starting the long trek back toward civilization.

Suddenly, Garrity felt an intense pain in his back. He yelled and staggered, falling down to his knees. The pain didn't subside, though. He jerked his pack off and grabbed for the spot on his back. His hand came away slick with blood.

What the hell? Garrity clutched at himself. There was something embedded in his back. He hissed as he pulled it out. Staring at the object, it took him a couple of seconds to realize what he was looking at. It was a tiny, golden dagger.

Garrity grabbed his pack and lurched to his feet. But the pack was empty. He looked inside, forgetting even the burning pain in his back for moment. The idol was gone. He cast about for it, trying to see if it could have rolled out somewhere nearby.

That was when the slash across his Achilles tendon sent him to the ground again. Garrity shrieked as the tendon rolled up like a cheap set of blinds. He flopped onto his back and grabbed at the second tiny dagger lodged in his leg.

He groaned and started to crawl away, dragging his useless leg behind him. He glanced back just long enough to catch a glimpse of a tiny, golden figure rush toward him out of the underbrush.

I still have access to the original files. I might be able to do something. Maybe I can fix some of this. I don't want to mess around with things after what happened last time. But maybe I can use a lighter touch. Maybe I can just bump things in the right direction.

FIFTY-FOUR
MAKEUP

Emily's standards tended to evaporate as the school year went on. At the start of the year, she wore plenty of makeup every day. Her hair was always nice, and she wore her professional shoes, the ones that pinched her toes.

That went out the window pretty quickly. By the time winter break rolled around a few months later, she wore whatever amount of makeup she thought was socially acceptable, her hair was a rat's nest if she didn't simply tie it up in a bun, and she wore her comfy shoes, which looked like hot crap.

There were exceptions, of course. She was prim and proper and fancy on picture day. Or the dreaded parent-teacher conference days. Or anytime she knew she had to ask the principal for something.

But most years, the kids were pretty successful at wearing her standards down to the nub within a couple of months. It wasn't just that she never seemed to have the time for anything more advanced than a quick touch up, though that was certainly a factor; it was the simple fact that she was just plain *tired*.

It took a lot out of her just to get them to sit still through math. Usually, there was an outbreak of pinching or noise making or general distractedness halfway through anyway, and it was like starting over from scratch. Actually getting the concepts to sink in was a Sisyphean task, though. She'd explain the lesson, have them practice, and discover that only two kids actually understood what they were supposed to be doing. Some of them would make progress, and then they'd seemingly forget everything by the next day.

It was especially bad with students like Kyle. That boy was a particularly frustrating combination of willfully ignorant and naturally slow. He wouldn't follow along with what she was teaching unless she hovered over him, and when Kyle did decide to tune in, he couldn't figure out what he was supposed to do without excruciatingly simple instructions just for him.

After all that, the little things like hair and makeup just seemed like too much. Aside from the basics, they fell by the wayside like so much dead weight.

Today, she actually felt pretty good as she stood in front of the mirror and worked at her makeup kit. It was one of those big days where she felt obligated to look her best, but things would be easier from here on out. She'd just had a full meal and things had finally started to come together in her classroom.

Using her makeup brush, she disguised the last row of scales still visible around her neckline and popped her false teeth in to hide her fangs. She eyed herself in the mirror one last time and decided that her human disguise was absolutely on point today. Now, she was truly ready for that meeting with the principal and the police about Kyle's disappearance. It still felt nice to get gussied up every once in a while.

I don't know about the ethics of this. I'm going to be screwing up somebody else's universe with this. Okay. Okay, let's see what the next one is. If it's bad, I'll see if I can change it. Maybe I can fix it.

DRAGON SLAYER

Sir Everett Harbottle drew his sword as he entered the cave. His armor glinted in the waning sunlight. Each step forward took him further into darkness. He moved cautiously, trying not to let his armor rattle and clatter as he walked. Even so, leather straps and bronze buckles groaned and clinked. The edges of his plate metal rubbed against his chainmail undershirt and leggings.

This was dangerous territory. Everett was under no illusions. If he was to find Princess Wilhelmina, he would almost certainly have to fight the dreadful beast guarding her. Perhaps he would find himself lucky, and the hulking creature would be asleep or away. But he wasn't counting on luck.

He tightened his grip on the sword hilt as he rounded a bend in the cave, finding a wide cavern. Parts of the grotto's roof had collapsed, allowing a few streamers of sunlight to filter down into the space.

Sir Everett had spoken with some of the peasants who tilled the nearby lands. A few of them had seen the dragon, if only briefly. Those who had gotten a better look were mostly dead.

They all described the same thing, though. A great and terrible beast, massive in size. It had fearsome claws that could rip open a house, and nigh impenetrable green skin. The monster had left a trail of devoured farm animals and chewed corpses in its wake.

Sir Everett would save Princess Wilhelmina from the dragon, though. Now that he'd discovered its lair, he had his best opportunity. He would save her from the clutches of the evil beast and win her hand in marriage in the process. His mighty sword, Wyrm's Bane was designed to slaughter dragons and wyverns. Its pommel was carved from dragon bone, and the edge was sharpened to carve through even the thickest hide.

He stepped in something. Lifting his armored foot, Sir Everett looked down at the ragged length of blood-stained satin. There were still bits of skin attached to it, matted there with sticky viscera. His heart sank in his chest. A weakness struck his knees, and it was all he could do to keep himself on his feet. Oh no. No, no, no.

Then, the culprit emerged from the shadows. The villagers had not led Sir Everett astray in most regards, but they had misunderstood a key detail.

The huge mantis clacked its claws together, its mouthparts caked in a crimson veil of gore. Sir Everett swung his weapon at the beast as it approached, but the blade bounced off the chitinous armor like a child's wooden sword.

The mantis snatched him up, its spiked forelimbs piercing through his armor as easily as fresh whey. Sir Everett swung his sword again, but the blade smashed against the smooth, hard exoskeleton like he was bashing a rock.

And then the gigantic insect's mouthparts were clicking and snipping, slicing through Sir Everett's armor and seeking out the soft flesh inside the hard shell, doing exactly what they were designed to do.

That was bad. That was real bad. Hold on. I'm going to try to change it. Hold on. Maybe I can solve it. Maybe it'll be better. Hold on. Just hold on. I'm going to tinker with the file.

DRAGON SLAYER

Sir Everett Harbottle drew his sword as he entered the cave. His armor glinted in the waning sunlight. Each step forward took him further into darkness. He moved cautiously, trying not to let his armor rattle and clatter as he walked. Even so, leather straps and bronze buckles groaned and clinked. The edges of his plate metal rubbed against his chainmail undershirt and leggings.

He felt an odd sense of déjà vu.

This was dangerous territory. Everett was under no illusions. If he was to find Princess Wilhelmina, he would almost certainly have to fight the dreadful beast guarding her. Perhaps he would find himself lucky, and the hulking creature would be asleep or away. But he wasn't counting on luck.

He tightened his grip on the sword hilt as he rounded a bend in the cave, finding a wide cavern. Parts of the grotto's roof had collapsed, allowing a few streamers of sunlight to filter down into the space.

And there was the princess! She lay on a pile of stone rubble, her arm over her face as she softly wept. She knew how deep a plight she was in.

She looked up at the sound of Sir Everett's approach. At the same time, there was a rumble from deeper within the cave, far back in the darkness.

"No!" Princess Wilhelmina shouted.

The dragon emerged from the shadows, its taloned feet scraping against the stone floor. Its obsidian scales glittered in the dying light. A pair of beady, red eyes focused on Sir Everett.

With a shriek like a wooden ship breaking apart on the rocky coast, the beast lunged forward. Everett dodged to the side, taking cover behind a rock formation. The creature's huge claws lashed against the stone, scoring the rock.

Everett circled around to the far side of the rock and found himself face-to-face with the titanic dragon. It opened its mouth, revealing a set of massive, recurved fangs. A glow blossomed to life in the back of its throat, kindling brighter and brighter. In a second, the dragon would spew fiery death down on Everett.

Lunging forward, Everett thrust his sword into the soft flesh on the underside of the dragon's neck. The creature screamed, the noise trailing off into a gurgle as Everett carved his sword downward, cutting through veins, tendons, and dark, oily meat. Hot, steaming blood, black as sin, jetted across the floor. The earth shook as the dragon lurched and collapsed in front of Everett, its last breaths spent choking on its own bile and bloody gorge.

Victorious, Everett strode toward the princess. She wept harder as he grabbed her and hoisted her up. Her pet and protector lay dead on the cavern floor.

Dusk had fallen over the land as Everett emerged. He lifted his visor plate, revealing a set of empty eye sockets. Bits of ancient, leathery skin clung to his skull. The only source of light came from the flaming remains of the village and the castle in the distance, dark clouds of smoke rising into the sky. Once he sacrificed the princess to his dark lord, Everett's victory would be truly complete.

That was worse. Oh crap. Wait. I'm going to try again. I don't know what I'm doing. Maybe if I reset it again?

FIFTY-FIVE
DRAGON SLAYER

Sir Everett Harbottle readied himself as he entered the cave. His plated armor glinted in the waning sunlight. Each step forward took him further into darkness. He moved cautiously, trying not to let his armor scrape against the stone as he walked.

He felt an odd sense of déjà vu.

This was dangerous territory. Everett was under no illusions. If he was to find his kidnapped love, he would almost certainly have to fight the dreadful beast guarding her. Perhaps he would find himself lucky, and the creature would be asleep or away. But he wasn't counting on luck.

He sniffed the air as he rounded a bend in the cave, finding a wide cavern. He could smell the rank odor of the dreadful beast. Parts of the grotto's roof had collapsed, allowing a few streamers of sunlight to filter down into the space.

And there was the princess! She lay on a pile of stone rubble, her arm over her face. She sat, apparently resting. Sir Everett stepped closer, and the princess stirred.

She looked up at the sound of Sir Everett's approach. At the same time, there was a rumble from deeper within the cave, far back in the darkness.

"No!" Princess Wilhelmina shouted.

The dragon emerged from the shadows, its taloned feet scraping against the stone floor. Its obsidian scales glittered in the dying light. A pair of beady, red eyes focused on Sir Everett.

Sir Everett stood firm. He had to rescue his love. He wouldn't allow anything to stand in his way, no matter the cost.

Princess Wilhelmina ran toward Sir Everett. Moving remarkably fast in her heels, she scrambled off the rocks.

But Sir Everett was faster yet. He swung his weapon around and drove it through the princess's chest. It punctured her ribcage and shot out her back with a noise like someone puncturing a waterskin. She gasped, a wet and sticky sound. Blood and viscera staining the princess's finery. The enchanted dagger in her hand fell to the ground. He reared back and blew a gust of fire over the bloodied form on the ground.

Sir Everett ran to his love. His forked tongue flicked in and out of his mouth, tasting the copper-scented air. The scaleless abomination was dead, and he was victorious. Books and vellum script lay near the dead woman's body. He'd killed the realm's foremost authority on dragon ecology and social structure.

He and his love rubbed their snouts together. He'd freed her from captivity in this awful cave. Tomorrow, the village and castle would burn in retribution.

The little changes aren't working. It's all falling apart. I don't know how many times I can keep doing this. What am I doing to these people? Okay. One more time. Just one more try. I'm going to do a bigger jump this time. A big jolt. Maybe I can reset it. Maybe I can force a happy ending to this story. If I can just fix one story, I should be able to fix mine when the time comes. Just don't let me die, okay? Here we go. One more try.

DRAGON SLAYER

Scarulex hid in the shadows in the darkest part of the cavern. She was fairly certain that she was the last one left alive. All the others had been murdered in cold blood, carved up like suckling pigs by that madman.

She huddled as far into the darkness as her large frame would allow. Her claws clicked and clacked on the rock. Her scaly hide rasped against the stone. Her hot, panicky breath sent tendrils of smoke puffing toward the ceiling.

She felt a terrible sense of déjà vu.

Hiding in the cave had been a mistake. This was obviously where the errant knight had been living. There were scraps of food around an old firepit, and the walls were covered in odd, sub-literate carvings.

There were pieces of dragon bodies everywhere. Scarulex saw Pentak's head laying on the ground in a puddle of black, oozing blood. The rest of the pieces she couldn't identify. But she had a dreadful suspicion that one of the bloodied, amputated claws nearby belonged to Meslar. The knight had butchered them all, each and every one of her friends.

And he'd brought parts of the bodies back here, arranging them in front of a pile of stony rubble as if offering them up to a god.

A single figure sat at the top of the rock formation. The skeleton wore a dress that had once been made from the finest cloth. Now, it was damp and rotten, clinging to the figure's leather-sheathed bones like another layer of decaying skin. Most of a head of long, flowing hair still clung to the figure's skull.

The dead princess had a few accoutrements laid around her. A brush. A cracked hand mirror. A couple of moldering books. It looked like Sir Everett had been bringing her offerings for years. The madman had been worshipping her. Or in love with her. Or bound by some crazed duty, warped and broken by a deranged mind. And then Scarulex and her friends had the misfortune to stumble into the mad knight's territory.

Suddenly, she heard something. A scratching, scraping noise. The sound grew louder, now accompanied by heavy, rattling footsteps.

After a moment, Sir Everett appeared in the mouth of the cave. He dragged his massively oversized sword behind him, the rusted, chipped blade spitting up sparks as it went. His pitted, scratched armor clung haphazardly to his huge but emaciated frame.

Scarulex held her breath as the murderer moved closer. He hadn't seen her in the shadows yet, though. He moved directly toward the pile of rubble and the dead princess. He clambered upward and sat next to her. Pulling open a satchel on his hip, he pulled out a hunk of raw, quivering dragon flesh. He lifted his helmet visor and took a big, hearty bite, chewing with gusto. Then, he offered the rest to the princess. When her bony arm didn't take it, he pressed it up to the skull's mouth, smearing it over her teeth. The blood the meat left behind looked like a harlequin's lipstick. He seemed confused that she didn't want his offering.

It was now or never. Sir Everett was distracted. Scarulex crept through the shadows, aiming for the cavern's exit. Then, her talons accidentally sent a small rock clattering across the floor. Sir Everett's head whipped around, his visor snapping down, and all Scarulex could see of his face was his deranged eyes staring directly at her. He sprang up, his gigantic sword in his grip as Scarulex ran.

Christ on a pogo stick.

FIFTY-SIX

BLACK PICKUP TRUCK

Randall put his hand on Velma's knee. "You ready?"

"Let's go," she said.

They hadn't made it very far out of their hometown yet, but the honeymoon was already shaping up to be a blast. It was Velma's idea to take a driving tour, seeing parts of the country they'd always wanted to see but never had the chance.

Randall checked his mirrors and twisted his head around to look through the rear window. He had to look past the "JUST MARRIED" soaped there. He backed out of the diner parking lot, full and happy and content. Velma looked beautiful, he was feeling refreshed, and they were still making great time. He'd just had a fantastic burger, maybe the best he'd ever eaten, and he was ready to hit the road again.

No sooner did Randall find his way back onto the highway before a big, black pickup truck raced up behind him. The truck came up close to his bumper, far too close for comfort. Randall didn't recognize the model, but he saw the driver waving frantically at him in his mirrors.

The truck honked at him. Honked again. And again. Several people had honked at Randall already on the trip, usually giving a friendly wave afterwards. They wanted to congratulate a stranger on a new marriage. People were pretty amicable in this part of the country. But the truck behind him didn't seem like it was here to be friendly.

"What does he want?" Velma asked, twisting around to look at the truck.

"Maybe we forgot something at the diner or something? Could be he wants to tell us something." Randall felt for his wallet and found its familiar weight right where it should be. Velma's purse sat by her feet. "Maybe I should pull over and see what he wants," Randall said.

He didn't want to, though. In fact, he didn't like the way the truck was following him so closely. He didn't like it one bit. It was too aggressive. The way the driver waved wasn't exactly frantic, but there was a weird vibe going on there.

Randall tapped his brakes, preparing to pull over just in case the other driver had something important to tell them. But then, the pickup truck pulled into the oncoming traffic lane, the driver's eyes glued on Randall's car. The truck pulled up next to Randall, and the other driver tried to shout something through the lowered passenger window.

That was when the oncoming big rig collided with the black truck.

***

"Well, I'm sorry you folks had to see that," the coroner said, looking at the young, married couple.

"Any idea who the guy was?" The husband scratched at his cheek as he looked back at the wreckage.

"Can't say we do. I'd advise that you folks put it out of your mind. It's my problem now. Doesn't sound like y'all did anything wrong. Just some reckless driver who wanted to race you. Maybe thought it would be funny to bother folks on their honeymoon for some knuckleheaded reason. The only person at fault is him. You go on now. Enjoy your honeymoon."

"Thank you. We will," the wife said.

The coroner watched them get back in their car and drive off. Then, he turned back to the scene. What was left of the driver lay under a sheet. The deputies had gathered all the pieces they could find from the road and the nearby field. A towing service had already collected the big rig, and the driver had been questioned and released.

They didn't know who the dead guy was. His driver's license had his name, Norman, but they were having trouble getting into contact with anyone who knew him. Normally, that would mean a quick trip to the potter's field.

But the coroner had a cousin who owned a diner down the way. Times were tough, and the diner mostly served travelers,

125

anyway. Just folks passing through, like the married couple. He and his cousin had a deal going.

"You boys can knock off," the coroner said to the remaining deputies. "Just get everything loaded in the car, and I'll take it from there."

FIFTY-SEVEN

DENTISTRY

A dental drill whined somewhere nearby. It was not a pleasant noise, high and tinny. Sid could hear the pitch change as it grated over someone's teeth in the other room.

The dentist leaned over him, his facemask obscuring everything but his eyes. He had a little light on a headband, almost like an old mining helmet, that half-blinded Sid.

"Open up, please," the dentist said, picking up a set of pointy, steel tools.

Sid did as he was asked. In some ways, he was glad to be here. He finally had insurance that covered trips to the dentist's office. But it was cheap insurance, and it only worked at this cut-rate place. In the other room, the dental drill continued its work, buzzing like an angry insect.

"My, my, my," the dentist said.

"Issa ad?" *Is it bad?* Sid tried to talk around the steel instruments probing his mouth.

"Let's see. I'm noticing a few things right away. Tell me, when was the last time you flossed?" The dentist took his tools out of Sid's mouth so he could speak.

"It's been a while."

"I can tell. I'm going do a quick floss on you while I continue looking everything over, all right? Open up again, please."

Sid stretched his mouth open as wide as it would go, and the dentist went in like a terrier after a rat. He could feel every poke and prod as the dentist worked.

"You have not one but two chipped teeth back here, there's bits of food caught everywhere, your canines are crooked in a way I've never seen outside a textbook, there's an abscess on your tongue that may or may not be threatening to become a sentient entity, several of your back teeth are absolutely black with rot, and at least three, no, four different clans of gum disease are staging a turf war in there," the dentist said.

"So, pretty good then, right?"

"Honestly, you're the best I've seen all week. We'll just have your teeth sharpened and send you on your merry way." The dentist pulled his facemask off and revealed a snout full of jagged fangs.

"Oh good. I was worried they'd all be pearly white," Sid said, re-hinging his jaw. "My old Monstrosium insurance didn't cover dental."

"No need to worry," the dentist said, tossing away the length of intestine he'd flossed Sid's teeth with. "We'll have you back out and ready to eat children within the hour."

FIFTY-EIGHT

KILL THE BEAST

Tybalt hefted a torch toward the night sky. "We must kill the creature," he bellowed.

Cheers erupted all around him. The other villagers held pitchforks and torches of their own. Dozens of fearful but energized faces gazed back at him from around the town square.

The bell tower rang, summoning the rest of the townsfolk to the courtyard outside the small church. He watched a few remaining peasants arrive, bringing whatever makeshift weapons they could gather. Even the town guard was present, wielding swords and cudgels.

The beast had already killed two huntsmen that had been dispatched after it, and now it had taken up refuge in the crumbling castle at the edge of the woods. Tybalt didn't know what hell the monster had crawled out of, but he intended to send it back. As far as he could tell, the creature primarily came out at night.

He gazed out at the crowd. There were still a few prominent faces missing. The local lord had apparently chosen to shelter in his chateaux with his personal guard, cowering behind his stone walls, no doubt. Ulric the merchant had been around earlier, selling "monster repellant tonic," but he'd vanished now that it was time to take action.

It was no matter. Tybalt had the numbers he needed. The common folk, the ones who had actually seen the abomination sneaking through their fields and skulking through the woods, would deal with the matter. The creature had a fearsome roar, and it could launch deadly quills, but it couldn't withstand the might and fury the whole village.

"We move on the castle," Tybalt shouted, leading the procession out of town. The crowd shifted, following him, ready for blood.

***

Major Hawkins clutched his little service pistol and watched the tentacled beings approach the stony hillfort where he'd taken shelter. Some of them wielded torches, and others held various crude weapons. Their hideous, gelatinous bodies pulsed with angry purpose.

Hawkins forced himself to tear his eyes away. He raced back to his damaged spaceship and grabbed his tools. He already knew that he couldn't repair the worst of the damage, though. He'd tried to go out and gather resources and materials he could use at night, but his presence had only antagonized the alien beings. Now, they were coming for him.

He heard the sound of something heavy crashing against the rotting doors, and he prepared to make his final stand.

FIFTY-NINE
LOVE LETTERS

Joey Sabatelli sat on the bed in his cell and ran his hands through his hair. He'd been doing it for hours. There wasn't anything better to do on death row, so why not?

"Aye, Joey. You got mail," one of the guards said.

"I don't want it."

"Well, throw it away yourself then. I ain't going to carry it around anymore." The mail came through the bars of his cell and landed on the floor. It was just as single letter.

Joey remembered when he used to get excited about mail. He sighed and hauled his tired bones off the bed. He bent down and picked the envelope off the floor. Slitting the envelope open with his index finger, her extracted the letter inside. The scent of perfume hit him like a bomb.

My dearest Joey…

This again. Joey didn't respond to any of the letters. A steady stream of them kept coming in, though. Lucinda Valdez would not be dissuaded.

Joey used to get letters from a few lonely ladies, especially right after his trial. It was a pretty common phenomenon, actually. A number of guys on death row, particularly the younger and handsomer ones, had their little fan clubs. Joey's had dwindled down until there was no one left but Lucinda, and he just wished she would go away.

I dream of holding you in my arms. I dream of holding your big, strong hands in mine. I can't wait to see you.

The guards read these. Joey assumed they snickered at them before passing them on. Lucinda didn't seem to mind that he never responded to her. She didn't seem to mind that he had been put in this hole for killing his wife and three children. Unlike some of the women who'd latched onto him right after his trial, she never once said that she believed he was innocent. In fact, she seemed all the more enamored because of his guilt.

I know we will be together in due time.

Joey had never responded for a simple reason. He had access to some computer time in here. He'd run Lucinda Valdez through every search engine he could find. The results always came back the same.

The top result was inevitably an old newspaper article titled *Hellbound Bride.* The old, old news story, dated almost a century ago, detailed the many crimes of one Lucinda Valdez. She'd killed some seven husbands over the course of ten years. She'd been executed in this very prison when the walls were still new and the original coat of paint still clung to the bars.

When you visit my neck of the woods in a few days, come find me. I'll be waiting for you.

Joey looked up at the calendar on his wall. The date three days from now was circled in red. All the days after that were crossed out. He crumpled the letter up and threw it in the trash.

His execution was imminent. He wasn't afraid of falling asleep after a little jab with the doctor's needle. But the letters knew things about him that they had no business knowing. They knew what he did in solitary confinement, where not even the guards' cameras could see in some of the corners.

He wasn't afraid of drifting off to sleep in the death chamber, but he was terrified he might wake up next to Lucinda Valdez. The letters were always sweet, but Joey had read about her crimes. He knew what happened to the men she was sweet on. And in death, there would be no escape.

SIXTY

SHOW AND TELL

Julia Deckard loved her students' weekly show and tell session. She could sit at her desk and get much-needed work done on her computer while her students showed off their little treasures. The process was simple enough that it mostly ran itself. Everyone sat in a circle and took turns presenting to the class.

She didn't have to referee much. Sometimes the boys would bring in a favorite action figure and she'd have to break up a "fight" on the sidelines between Batman and a tyrannosaurus, but mostly she just tried to make sure that everyone received a roughly equal amount of time. Thanks to a little timer on her desk, that wasn't hard to accomplish.

Sometimes the kids even brought in genuinely interesting stuff. Lily brought in a *Minié* ball bullet one time, a family heirloom from a great-great-grandfather who fought in the Civil War. Julia wouldn't have trusted one of her youngsters with anything so cool. She'd seen Lily get a crayon stuck up her nose once. No, twice.

But it was still a welcome bit of history in the classroom.

The other items kids brought in ranged the gamut. Battle Monster trading cards. Grumpy hamsters. A cool rock that turned out to be an owl pellet one time. Everything had to go in a special bin after show and tell, nominally so that no one would lose their special trinket but mostly so the kids wouldn't get distracted and play with whatever they brought in during actual learning time.

The timer on Julia's desk chirped and Julia quickly reset it.

"Okay, Zack. Thanks for sharing your stuffed dog with us."

"His name is Stinky!" Zack said, beaming back at her.

Julia already knew that. Zack had been very proud of his great wit while telling the rest of the kids about Stinky. Julia simply refused to acknowledge it.

"Austin, what did you bring to share with us this week?" Julia asked, already turning most of her attention back to the spreadsheet on her screen.

The little boy gave her a big smile and pulled the prostitute's severed head out of his bag by the hair. Blood and smeared makeup had turned the woman's face into a garish clown mask of horror, her final, ghastly grimace still plastered on her face.

"I found this in Daddy's basement," Austin said, proud as could be.

Julia squinted at an email from the principal. Something about a parent being arrested. She said what she always said when she wasn't paying attention.

"Uh-huh. Pass it around for the class to see."

SIXTY-ONE
SPECIAL FORCES

Hal Overbeck laced up his combat boots. From a very early age, he knew he wanted to join the military. In his youth, he started out bashing army men action figures together in the name of freedom. Later, he graduated to practicing his aim with a squirrel gun, what his father affectionately referred to as a "varmint popper," in the woods behind his home.

Now, he was a commissioned officer in an elite unit. He couldn't have been more proud. His childhood self would think he was outrageously cool, which was never a bad goal to have in life. He was part of a top-notch special forces unit, leading the fight.

The life wasn't exactly what he was expecting, though. That was probably true of every profession. Law students were probably surprised by the first time they set foot in a real courtroom. Medical students were probably surprised the first time they were left to their own devices in a hospital setting. Hell, the kids who wanted to grow up to be garbage men were probably in for some surprises behind the wheel of those big trucks.

But this was different. Covert raids straight into the bowels of hell. Defending against surprise assaults. Counseling the grunts in the main infantry line.

He'd seen men blown apart, burned to blackened skeletons, and injured in any number of horrific ways. Imagining it when he was a kid, it was all heroics and valiant final charges, and anyone who died did so at the top of a hill with great drama and fanfare. Instead, he'd seen a lot of distinctly inglorious ways to die. He was the tip of the spear, a trained killing machine, but there was a lot of ugliness in this war. It was a calling.

Hal grabbed his kit. It was time to head out into the breach again. Another patrol in the combat zone. He said a little prayer and packed the last magazine of silver bullets and bottles of holy water.

The SEALs, the Green Berets, Delta Force. None of them had a thing on the Chaplain Corps for bringing the fight to the enemy since the demon portals opened.

SIXTY-TWO
WHAT IS IT, GIRL?

Henry sat on a log, getting ready to stick his bait on the hook, when Midge burst through the bushes and barked at him. Midge was a beautiful dog, a big collie with light markings. He'd inherited her from his uncle, who used to have a small ranch down in the southern part of the state.

The old dog had faced something of a hard life. That was just as true for animals as it was for people out on the frontier. She'd answered to a few different masters over the years. One fell down an old well. Another got caught in some machinery at a mill. Henry's uncle had drowned. Life was short out here beyond the bonds of civilization. But every frontiersman had use for a good dog, and Midge was one of the best. She was smart as a whip and quick to learn routines, which made her a useful companion.

Midge barked again and looked up at Henry.

"What is it, girl?"

Midge barked again. She disappeared back into the bushes for a second and reemerged with Caroline's bonnet. Henry stared at his daughter's dirty, slightly tattered bonnet for a moment. He'd left her inside the cabin, well away from any immediate danger. This part of the countryside was relatively free of wolves, bears, or hostile tribes. But Henry had seen tragedy before in these lands. It was a too common experience for the frontiersmen and homesteaders who had travelled this far west.

Icy fear suddenly gripped his heart. Caroline was all he had. The little girl was sweet and precocious, and she was growing up into a fine young lady. After his wife succumbed to the fever, Caroline became his everything.

"Take me to her," Henry said. Midge dropped the bonnet and raced off, Henry close behind her.

His heart sank further when Midge ran past the cabin rather than to it. She dashed up the trail into the hills behind the cabin, moving with purpose. His breath came in a steady rhythm, and he had a stitch in his side as he followed Midge up the switchbacks to the top of the overlook, but he ignored everything. Henry called Caroline's name, but he got no response.

Midge stopped at the edge of the cliff and looked down. His heart beat hard in his chest, not just from the mad dash up the hill, but from the sudden awful dread that had overtaken him. Bracing himself, Henry stepped closer and looked over the side of the steep rock formation.

That was when the dog bumped into him from behind.

Midge watched the body roll and tumble down the sheer wall of stone before landing with a heavy thud at the bottom. She sat and wagged her tail. Eventually, she would alert someone about the accident, and lead the authorities to the body. Then, they would shower her with praise and treats. Midge was a smart girl and quick to learn routines.

SIXTY-THREE
ZZZZZZZZZZZZZZZZZZ

As far as Geoffrey Klein knew, he was the last surviving person on earth. There were possibly more people elsewhere, but he had no idea how to contact them or reach them. His little research station in northern Greenland might very well be the last bastion of the human race. Unfortunately, he was almost out of food, and he had no means to come by more.

The virus had destroyed humanity. It seemed as though the threat had spread across the world almost as soon as it was identified. The undead numbered in the billions, seemingly everywhere all at once. There was no escape, and they left behind bodies, stripped of flesh and muscle, everywhere they went. They devoured everything that moved, eating indiscriminately.

Geoffrey heard plenty of debate over whether or not the things were technically alive or not over his radio. Researchers in various fields from other stations in Greenland had chimed in at various points, offering their two cents on the matter. They'd all either moved on or died now. Their radio transmissions were all silent.

Geoffrey eyed the few remaining cans in his pack. Then, he peeked outside. There was a dark cloud on the horizon. He eyed the cloud and sighed.

The inhospitality of the environment had kept him alive here so far. Everything was either ice or stone, save for a few hardy strands of lichen here and there. The cruel wind and crushing cold lashed the life out of everything else that tried to take root here. That had kept him isolated, a hermit on the edge of the world, and it had spared him. Now, it would condemn him. He had to pack his sled and start moving south toward the ruins of Nuuk, the former capital city. He expected to meet his end before he arrived.

When he was younger, he liked to read stories about the zombie apocalypse. It seemed ridiculous now to be fascinated by such things, especially since the real event had been so different. His teenage self, who had spent hours formulating the ultimate undead

138

escape plan, would have been chewed to bits in minutes upon encountering the real horde.

It was the insects. The disease spread through them like wildfire. One million trillion individual ants, wasps, beetles, and flies, all seeking whatever blood and flesh they could find. Together, they far outweighed the collective mass of the human race, and they crashed across the cities in veritable tsunamis of chitin and pincers.

He eyed the dark cloud on the horizon again. The insects, dead and hungry, were growing closer. Their low, droning buzz filled the air until it was the only thing he could hear.

SIXTY-FOUR
SUMMONING RITUAL

Night fell over the graveyard.

"I have everything I need for the ritual," Erasmus said.

Don't be so dramatic Lisa wanted to say but didn't. The night was dark, and a mist had started to rise. The headstones stuck up above the ground fog like rocky shores waiting to smash unwary ships.

"And you think this will work?" Lisa asked instead. She didn't want to piss Erasmus off. Not now. This was their big chance.

"Oh, I *know* this will work. I absolutely guarantee that this will summon them. I've gathered everything we need to pierce the veil of the spirit world and bind them to us," Erasmus said, gesticulating wildly.

Erasmus deposited the materials he'd collected and arranged them in front of the gravestone. Lisa followed him, growing increasingly anxious as Erasmus finished constructing his little votive repository.

Lisa didn't have nearly the level of occult knowledge Erasmus did, but she knew Erasmus. Most of what he was doing was for the theater of it all rather than for effect. She knew enough that the summoning ritual wasn't actually that complicated. Psh. *Summoning ritual.* That was another of Erasmus's little grandiosities. It was a beacon. A lure. Their future spectral wards couldn't help but be drawn to it.

If you knew what you were doing, it wasn't that hard to create a thrall from the other side of the spirit realm. After careful research, they'd decided to summon a man named Gideon Manchester.

Even if she didn't particularly enjoy Erasmus's more flamboyant tendencies, it would all be worth it in the end. Incredible power would belong to them. Bending the line between life and death would present them with all manner of opportunities. With the full moon hanging over the graveyard, the time was finally right.

Erasmus scratched a match to life and touched it to the side of the little structure he'd built. After a few moments, the fire began to spread, slowly consuming the arrangement of items and wafting black smoke up into the night. The summoning ritual had begun. Gideon Manchester would be theirs to command.

After a few minutes, with the pyre growing in heat and intensity, a siren began to wail in the distance. A firetruck pulled up in front of the graveyard, and a group of firefighters spilled out and hooked up their hoses. Within minutes, they were blasting the pile of tires and smoldering garbage with water.

Fire Chief Gideon Manchester pulled up in a red truck. He walked up to the pile of scorched and melted trash.

"Damn kids," he muttered to himself, looking at the petty act of vandalism. The gravestones by the fire, marking the final resting places of a couple named Erasmus and Lisa, were blackened with soot.

Suddenly, a chill unlike anything he'd felt before crept over the fire chief. He jerked, and his fingers spasmed. Then, he went unnaturally still.

"You all right, chief?" One of the firefighters looked at Gideon quizzically.

"Never better," Gideon said in a strange voice.

The ritual was complete.

SIXTY-FIVE

PROTECTOR

Krajowski walked through the field with a pistol, his followers doing the rest of the cleanup. A zombie, its legs shattered by the landmines Krajowski had laid around the settlement the night before, crawled toward him. He popped it in the head with his pistol and kept moving.

He was proud of the little bastion he'd carved out. Several hundred people now resided behind the walls he'd built, safe from the ravenous dead. Relatively safe, at least.

They had enough supplies to last for a few more months. They could eke out some sort of existence by farming a small plot of land and collecting rain water. A couple of the survivors even had a plan to get their hands on a generator and get some electricity up and running. A lot of people missed having anything other than candles and torches at night.

Krajowski hadn't approved that plan yet, but he was leaning toward authorizing it. If they could get some lights up and running, it would attract more survivors from near and far. He knew there were at least a few other encampments nearby, and he'd love to absorb their manpower. There was safety in numbers, after all. There were other benefits to having more people, too. His group had taken losses, losses that he would be hard pressed to replace. He needed more bodies to man the barricades and keep watch, among other things. Consolidating the other groups was a long-term goal, though.

For now, the most important thing was keeping his own people alive and un-zombified. He shot another ghoul in the head as it crawled toward his boots.

Krajowski was the undisputed leader of his little band of survivors, a shepherd to this flock. He was their protector in these dark times, and he'd be damned if he'd suffer unnecessary attrition. He and his people would weather this zombie plague.

He looked around but he didn't see any more of the ghouls near the walls. That meant they were free to send a scouting party out to gather supplies. They needed more food.

For that matter, Krasjowski needed food, too. That was why he was doing all this in the first place. As a vampire, he couldn't feed off the zombies. Their blood was coagulated and disease-ridden in their veins. The people under his watch tolerated his infrequent depredations in exchange for the safety of his encampment. It was like throwing the occasional virgin into a volcano. They had a lottery in place to ensure fairness, and those with the most valuable skills were exempted.

But that was why Krasjowski was all the more eager to get some lights up and running. He needed to add to his flock.

<u>SIXTY-SIX</u>
SCARECROWS

Randall pulled the car over to the side of the road. Dust billowed up as his wheels churned into the gravel. Some of it clung to the soaped on "JUST MARRIED" on the back windshield. The cornfields stretched onward, seemingly forever. Velma looked up from the book she was reading.

"Oh, hell no," she said.

"That's kind of weird, don't you think?" Randall said pointing to the scarecrows lining the side of the road.

The scarecrows hung from their posts like defeated sentinels. Their raggedy clothes clung to their bodies, stuffing poking out through shirt sleeves and pantlegs. Long brimmed hats hung from their heads, shielding their faces.

The faces and the heads were something else altogether. A few of them seemed to be carved from old jack-o-lanterns. They'd shriveled and collapsed in on themselves in the intervening months, rotting into hideous caricatures. Other heads were made from the skulls of various livestock. Sheep. Pigs. Horses. Dogs. Unidentifiable things. The pumpkins and the skulls alike boiled with hungry flies.

There weren't just a few of the scarecrows, either. There were dozens. Maybe hundreds. They emerged from the rows of corn like tigers sliding out of the jungle toward a village. They stood so close to the road that they were in danger of being struck down by a wide truck. They squatted on short poles, gazing out at travelers' tires. They hung from tall, spindly poles like medieval prisoners who had been gibbeted for the public to see. They stood in conspiratorial clusters or by themselves.

"We're not far from the next town. Let's keep going," Randall said.

"Nope. Nope, nope, nope. We're taking the last nope train out of Nopeville, Randall. Turn this car around. I've seen movies with this stuff. We're taking another route."

"But we'll have to backtrack nearly an hour to get to the junction again," Randall said.

"You're going to drive this car to the damn moon, if that's what it takes. Turn us around before we get murdered by a corn cult or something."

Grumbling to himself, Randall twisted the wheel around to begin the long trek back. Velma was still a little shook up from the incident with the black pickup truck, and he didn't want to upset her any more. He checked his mirror one last time, eyeing the silent army of scarecrows disappearing behind them. He'd never admit it, but maybe Velma was right. That was creepy as hell.

***

Kortalan would never admit it, but maybe Vardaz was correct. He stroked his chin with one of his tentacles. Vardaz had observed that the Earth creatures kept even the cleverest flying beasts at bay with a simple inanimate automaton.

Since he and his shipmates landed and took over the tiny habitation center, they'd been determining how to keep more Earth creatures from entering their new center of operations. Kortalan had suggested a grid of directed energy weapons. Vardaz had noticed the crude homunculi around the nutrition fields and suggested they portended dread and doom for the creatures of this world. As preposterous as the plan seemed, the scarehumans were remarkably effective. No one yet knew of the alien beachhead on this planet.

SIXTY-SEVEN
MOVING TRUCK

Tyrone grunted as he heaved yet another box into the back of the truck. This was getting old fast.

Usually, when people moved house, they had boxes of every shape and size and weight. They had locations and items marked on the side in permanent marker. Kitchen – plates. Bedroom – books. Garage – Ken's stuff. That was the usual pattern anyway.

Tyrone had been a moving man for years, and he'd seen a lot of different systems in place. He liked to think he could tell a lot about the people moving based on how they had their items divvied up. Sometimes, he could tell that somebody was getting a divorce, one person hastily grabbing all their stuff and getting it out of there as fast as they could. Sometimes, he could tell that somebody was in the process of moving in with a partner, which was similar to the divorce process but generally more organized. Most of the time, he honestly had no idea what motivated the people whose stuff he was hauling, but he liked to guess. Starting a family and needed a bigger house. Maybe they got a better job in a new city. Maybe they'd found their dream home. Tyrone didn't get to find out. He was just here to get their crap from Point A to Point Z.

But this job was just weird. The boxes were all the same size, long and low. As far as he could tell, there weren't any labels, written or printed, anywhere on the cardboard. This looked more like an industrial delivery shipment than the typical house moving. The fact that the boxes were all the same size made it easy to Tetris them into the truck, but the damn things were heavy.

Tyrone wheeled his dolly around and went back in to the little suburban home to get another box. His back grumbled at him, and he had some sweat collecting around his armpits, but he'd worked worse jobs. He didn't like it when the homeowners stayed behind and shepherded everything out the door like he was planning to steal everything they owned.

He grabbed one of the last remaining boxes and worked the lip of the dolly under the edge. Time to stand it up and wheel it out.

Then, he got his footing and heaved. But his hands were sweaty. His fingers slipped. The box tumbled out of his grip and crashed on the floor, the cardboard flaps falling open.

Tyrone cringed. This wasn't the first box he'd ever dropped. He'd been expecting a crashing noise. Or the crunch of something fragile. It was always the fragile boxes that fell.

But no. There was just the sound of something heavy and solid. Tyrone peaked over the far side of the box. He'd just shove whatever it was back in and tape up the flaps again, like this incident never even happened.

The objcct was a body. Two bodies, actually. He spotted another one still mostly inside the box. One man was completely desiccated, as if he'd been dead for a very long time. The other men were fresher but still partially mummified. It looked like all their blood and been drained, and his organs had been yanked out like carrots from a garden. They were both wearing jumpsuits, a red one and a blue one. The jumpsuits had two different logos on them, logos for moving companies.

That was when he heard the footsteps sneaking up behind him and realized that he wasn't alone in the house.

SIXTY-EIGHT
POWDER

"All right, show me what you got," Trevor said, sitting down on the cheap, stained hotel couch. Outside the window, the sun was setting on the Miami skyline.

Esteban clicked open his briefcase and revealed several bags full of pale powder. He waved a hand at the cache like a gameshow model showing off a fabulous prize.

"Aw yeah. That's the stuff." Trevor rubbed his hands together.

"There's more where that came from," Esteban said.

"How much?"

"I can have two truckloads here by noon tomorrow, if you have the funds."

Trevor whistled. "I'm good for it. We've been working together long enough that you ought to know that by now." He pulled a duffle bag up onto the couch and unzipped it. Stacks of cash were barely visible inside.

Esteban glanced inside and the bag and smiled. "It seems we have a deal, then. Would you like to sample the goods to make sure you're happy with them?"

"Hell to the yeah, my man." Trevor took one of the baggies out of Esteban's suitcase and pinched a bit of the powder directly onto the hotel table. Not too much. He didn't want to get greedy. Prices had been going up, and he had quotas to meet. That didn't mean he didn't enjoy the nose candy too, though.

He reached into his duffle bag and peeled a hundred-dollar pill off one of the stacks. Benjamin Franklin looked up at him disapprovingly. Trevor rolled the bill into a little tube, bent over the table, and snorted up a line of the powder.

The effect was instantaneous. Little fireworks went off inside his skull. Memories that weren't even his blinked on in his brain. It was like Frenching the grim reaper.

Trevor had been an accountant once. He got into the stuff shortly after his grandfather died, and he never looked back. This paid a lot better, and he knew all the tax and number tricks to keep the feds off his back. The folks dealing in cocaine had no idea what they were missing.

"Hell yeah," Trevor said, life coursing through his veins. He dropped the money back in the bag and pushed it toward Esteban. He pulled out a hanky. A dribble of blood ran out of his nose and mixed with the dust on his upper lip.

Esteban merely pushed the briefcase toward Trevor, the logo for the local crematorium printed on the side.

SIXTY-NINE

CHOP CHOP

Monica felt sweat drip down her forehead, but she didn't have time to wipe it away.

"You have ten seconds left," the cooking contest host said. Out of the corner of her eye, she could see the oversized buzzer counting down. She grabbed the steaks off the tray and tossed them on the plates as the host began counting down.

Monica had already made it through the contest's first round. Yesterday, she didn't expect to make it through the audition process, but here she was. The cameramen buzzed around her like oversized insects, capturing the final moments of her preparations. She had just enough time to drizzle some sauce over the plates before the alarm went off.

"Everyone, hands off your food," the host said.

Looking down at her plates, Monica grimaced. The steaks were slightly undercooked. They were still edible. They weren't exactly mooing anymore, but they hadn't cooked the way she'd expected, either. She'd simply run out of time to get the kind of sear she wanted. Biting her lip, she finally wiped the sweat off her face. Her heart beat faster as the crew took her plates over to the judges and took some glamour shots of finished meal.

Hundreds, maybe thousands, of people would be watching this.

She glanced over at her competitors. Simon looked about as frazzled as she did. He had some sort of sauce smeared on his apron from an unfortunate spill. There was a splatter mark up near his hairline that he evidently hadn't noticed yet. One of the makeup people kept trying to flag him down to fix it, but his eyes wouldn't stray from the plates of food being carried toward the judging table.

On her other side, Mark looked obnoxiously confident. He had a big, shiny earring dangling from one ear and a smug smile on his lips. He mugged for the cameras a bit, holding a plate up like it was a baby. He glanced over toward Monica, gave a pointed look at her food, and then drew a finger across his throat. The cameras got that from a couple different angles. Great.

Monica had some cooking experience, but the contest was infinitely harder than she expected. The kitchen was cramped, the lights were hot, and the countdown timer went far too fast.

Simon's food was critiqued first, but Monica barely heard a word from the judges. Then, it was her turn. The judges made a point of finding something good to say about her meal. They liked how she'd utilized some of the provided ingredients. But they all piled on when it came to the steak being too rare. She nodded and didn't make a fuss. They were right, and she didn't want to argue and antagonize them. The cameras lost interest in her as the judges turned their attention to Mark and his shiny earring.

She didn't hear most of what they said to him, either. She was too far in her own head, too tired to listen to anything that didn't directly impact her. Most of all, she just didn't want to be eliminated.

After conferring among themselves for a while, the judges reached their consensus. The lead judge looked directly into the camera to announce his decision.

"Mark, we're sorry, but your crème anglaise was flat, and it clashed far too much with the rest of your dish. You won't be heading to the next round."

Mark's eyes almost bugged out of his head as the cameramen closed in around him. A moment later, he was escorted away.

Monica let out a big sigh of relief, but she knew she couldn't relax too much. The next round was about to begin. Shockingly fast, a new cart of ingredients was wheeled out. With a flourish, the host pulled a sheet off the ingredients they had to use, handing the trays to Monica and Simon.

Monica's meat tray had a big, shiny earring in the middle of it. The cameras got a good angle on it as the heavily tattooed host chortled. One of the judges gave a big, involuntary twitch and continued mumbling to himself. Somewhere outside the insane asylum, the authorities were receiving a live feed of the proceedings.

This was how the inmates had chosen to eliminate their hostages if their demands weren't met. The timer started counting down again, and Monica grabbed her tray.

SEVENTY

A WORD FROM OUR SPONSORS

Where there's a will, there's a way. It's not just a mantra; it's a creed. Here at S.C. Sleep Supplies, it's our motto. It's what drove us to create our best pillow yet, the Divine Comfort.

We spent years engineering the perfect pillow, and we believe our newest model achieves that goal. Lovingly built by hand at our facility in South Carolina, these Divine Comfort Pillows are made with a patented combination of next generation memory foam materials and soft, pliable padding.

S.C. Sleep Supplies guarantees that you'll love our new Divine Comfort Pillow. The carefully selected materials mold perfectly to the sleeper's head, cradling them in place. Our unique materials provide the correct amount of airflow to ensure that the pillow retains the perfect shape, even after tossing and turning.

Where there's a will, there's a way. We spent almost twenty years perfecting our unique design to bring you the perfect Divine Comfort experience. Not only is our pillow perfect for any occasion, but it's compact and easy to store in even the most cramped bedroom, so it'll be ready to use at a moment's notice.

Rich relatives who already have everything? The Dive Comfort Pillow is perfect! Fussy children who don't want to go to sleep? The Divine Comfort Pillow is perfect! A spouse who spends all night snoring? The Divine Comfort Pillow is perfect! S.C. Sleep Supplies stands behind our products one hundred percent, and we know you'll love the results you get from our product.

Where there's a will, there's a way. It's our motto. It's our instructions to you. Here at S.C. Sleep Supplies, we make comfort affordable for those who are determined, for the doers and the shakers. With the Divine Comfort Pillow, you'll be ready to face any day.

As soon as the will is rewritten to include you more favorably, Smotherer's Choice Sleep Supplies will send you your brand-new Divine Comfort Pillow, and you'll be on your way to the best sleep of your life.

SEVENTY-ONE

CERTAIN LINEAGES

"And this process is…GMO-based?" Helen Birchfield asked the Dimshire Agriculture representative. The paper had sent her here to the so-called press conference to cover the announcement. She had a pen in her hand, ready to jot down more information. So far, the notebook was mostly filled with doodles. She didn't want to be here on a farm, for an agriculture industry event. She regretted complaining to her editor about covering the traffic accident beat.

"Absolutely not," the Dimshire representative said, the look on her face suggesting that Helen had just asked if anyone in her family liked to get freaky with goats. "This process is completely, one hundred percent organic. We've merely used selective breeding with certain lineages to greatly improve the robustness of our stock."

"Ah," Helen said. She still wasn't sure how she was going to get a story out of this. Dimshire Agriculture talked a big game, but a lot of it just sounded like fluff and re-branding to Helen.

The Dimshire representative had mentioned things like ending world hunger and restructuring the meat industry. Helen wasn't an expert in the field. She couldn't tell what was puffery and what was total crap. Her reporter instincts had her leaning toward total crap, though. Dimshire had been very coy with their details so far, so they were either building up toward a surprise, or they just wanted to waste everyone's time and get some free press.

The representative pointed to another reporter, someone from an industry specialty publication, when an alarm went off. Several red lights flashed overhead. A couple of men in suits ran into the conference hall and slammed the doors shut behind them. Someone caught on the other side of the doors pounded on them for a second, shouting bloody murder, then ran off. The representative went very pale behind the lectern.

"We have a breach!" One of the men waved to the representative. He had a streak of blood on his face.

Helen's first instinct was fire. She looked around for the exits, but the men in suits were barring the other doors. Terrorist attack? Natural disaster? What the hell was going on?

Suddenly, something huge hit the other side of the main doors. The wood splintered inward, opening up holes in the door. It looked like someone had smashed an axe into the doors. A few of the other reporters or trade specialists gasped or screamed.

Then, the doors burst inward off their hinges. A gigantic figure shoved its way into the room, standing almost ten feet tall. It was covered in gore-crusted feathers and fuzz. Massive, scaly feet kicked at the debris on the floor. The hulking dinosaur clucked once, and then it charged into the crowd.

SEVENTY-TWO

MOTE

Randall pulled the car into the parking lot. "I think this where we're going to be spending the night," he said. They were over an hour from the next town, and night had overtaken them quite a while ago. He didn't particularly like driving on these winding, mountain roads in the dark. All he could see were the outlines of trees and jagged peaks against the starry sky. They'd lost a lot of time backtracking earlier, and he was tired and cranky. In the darkness, the soaped on "JUST MARRIED" on his rear window practically glowed in the dark.

"I'm not sure I like the looks of this," Velma said from the passenger seat.

"I mean, it's not much, but I'm going to need a break soon," Randall said, stretching his back. His butt was numb after spending too long in the car. Not the best start to their honeymoon road trip.

The motel stood among the woods in the craggy butte. Randall could see the heaped outline of the mountain directly behind the structure, rising up toward the sky.

A neon sign blinked above the structure. It was supposed to read "MOTEL," but a letter had burned out. Now it simply read "MOTE." Beneath that, luminescent orange letters burned in the night. *Vacancy.*

"It's too isolated. I don't like it," Velma said. "Can't we just drive into the next town? I'd be fine even with a cheap chain hotel."

"The next town's pretty far," Randall said. He eyed the motel. He didn't see any additional signage. It was simply named MOTEL. Or rather, MOTE. There were only a couple other cars in the parking lot. They were both quite dirty, probably from driving through this area's rural mountain roads. That was why there was so much dust on them.

"Ever read *Psycho*? This looks like a murder trap if I ever saw one," Velma said. She hugged her arms around herself and looked over at Randall. Then she made that face. Randall was powerless to say no to that face.

He sighed. "Fine. We'll keep going."

"Thank you, Randall."

He circled around the parking lot, cruising tantalizingly close to the building and the rest it offered. None of the lights were on in any of the rooms. Then, he was back on the road, aiming for the horizon.

A few moments later, the craggy mass behind the motel shifted and stirred. A single, gigantic eye, as green and reflective as a jungle cat's, watched the car's taillights disappear in the distance. The massive shape behind the hotel settled in and waited, camouflaged and hungry.

More would come.

SEVENTY-THREE
JEWELRY

Flora walked between the stalls at the flea market. She wasn't interested in most of what she saw. Some of it was too expensive. A lot of it was crap. Some pieces were too beat up. More of it was labeled incorrectly. There were a couple of people trying to market fake gem stones as the real stuff. Maybe Flora wasn't enough of an expert to tell artificial diamonds from the real deal, but some of the pieces looked like they came out of quarter machines from the strip mall.

Then, something caught her eye. The stall was mostly empty but for a few items. Most of the jewelry pieces there weren't of any better quality than the stuff she'd already passed up.

But there was a pair of earrings with lovely green gemstones.

Flora walked up to the table, consciously trying not to look too interested in anything. She didn't want to look like she was salivating over any one particular item.

An older lady with glasses that looked like linked magnifying glasses sat behind the table. She nodded to Flora.

"Hi. Looking for anything special?"

"Just browsing," Flora said. Really, the earrings with the green stones were the only thing on the table worth buying. There wasn't that much there to begin with.

"If you're interested in anything in particular. Just ask."

"What about this?" Flora pointed to a cheap ring. "What kind of fitting is this?"

"Well, to be perfectly honest, I don't know. I'm selling this stuff on behalf of a family friend. She had to be institutionalized, and her family asked me to help raise some funds by selling off some of her items. If you're interested in the ring, I can give it to you for, say, fifty dollars."

The ring probably was not worth that much, and Flora wasn't interested in it in the first place. She just wanted to test the waters, to see how badly the old lady wanted to gouge her potential customers.

"What about these earrings?" Flora asked. "What sort of stone is this?"

"Again, I'm afraid I really don't know. If you like them, they're also fifty dollars."

Now that was a good deal. Flora was genuinely curious what the stone was, though. She'd never seen anything quite like it. That probably meant that it was some sort of fancy new artificial gem, but she rather liked it anyway. Maybe she'd have it appraised. If it turned out to be junk, she'd keep it. If it was valuable, she might just resell it at an appropriate price.

"I'll take them," she said.

****

A light flashed onscreen. The mothership whirred to life, its occupants gathering round the main display.

"The tracking beacon is moving again," one of them said, tentacles wriggling in fascination.

Their captain typed commands into the central console. "We'll move to acquire the new specimen at an appropriate time. Science team, I want you to keep this one's mind intact longer than the last one. We still have much to learn about this planet, and it won't do if the ear tag keeps transferring from subject to subject. Understood?"

It's me. George again. Yeah. Still here. I'm pretty defeated at this point. This was supposed to be my story. I used my access to the files to move my story out of the way.

SEVENTY-FOUR
ROMAN BATHS

Tiberius reclined in his luxurious tub. It was good to be governor, even of a remote and backwards eastern province such as this. The stresses of carrying out the emperor's will in these hinterlands were many, but the benefits were great as well. He was practically an emperor unto himself here, answering to no one except for the occasional heralds from distant Rome.

He had access to many luxuries, and he could pick items from the merchants' trade routes with impunity. What good was enormous worldly power if he couldn't abuse it a little? Despite his access to such bounty, his greatest pleasure was still a hot bath, though.

The practice of building large, public baths around warm springs hadn't reached this part of the world yet, but Tiberius had discovered something better. A private bath was a truly splendid experience.

Well, not completely private. A number of servants, including Carinus, remained nearby, ready to attend to his needs and to clean the tub when he was finished with it. Plus, he could call in any number of nubile, young local girls when he wanted the liquid warmed up a little.

He wriggled his toes in the tub, testing the temperature. He liked his baths warm, roughly body temperature. His current bath was beginning to cool down. Eventually, he needed to get back to the work of administering the realm, but he could spend a little longer in his tub.

Tiberius raised his hand above the edge of the tub and snapped. It wasn't a very loud snap, since his fingers were wet and dripping, but Carinus was by his side instantly. They knew better than to ignore him.

"Carinus, bring me a girl to freshen my bath, please."

The servant nodded trotted to the pair of massive doors at the end of the room. He returned with a young woman in tow, pulling her along by the arm.

Her eyes were wide as she looked around the opulent room, gazing around at the many trinket, baubles, and curios Tiberius had accrued in his position here. Her eyes fell on the governor, and she gasped. Evidently, Carinus had not told her to expect the governor lounging in his bath. Carinus pulled her over to the edge of the tub.

The woman tried not to look at him, but she stumbled through some broken Latin. "My lord, please. Is there anything I can do for you?"

"Freshen the bath, please."

"Of course, my lord. I'll just go and-"

"Not you," Tiberius said.

Carinus grabbed the woman by the hair and wrenched her head back. He used his knife to slash open her throat. Hot blood gushed out into the tub, spraying Tiberius in the process.

Not too cold. Not too hot. Just right. Tiberius sighed and sank down into the warm tub full of blood, cozy and happy again.

I didn't want to do that. I didn't want to put somebody else in harm's way. But I tossed that lady under the bus. Everyone who dies after this, it's at least partly my fault.

SEVENTY-FIVE

UNDEAD

Audrey stood her ground as the dead woman lurched forward. The walking corpse had long, dark hair that Audrey could tell had been cut by an expensive stylist once upon a time. Blood had matted some of the hair to her face, and she had sticks and old leaves and flecks of meat stuck in the remains of her hairstyle. She had a raw bald spot on one side where some of the hair had been ripped off her scalp. It looked like she'd been smacked in the side of the head with a brick at some point.

The zombie woman staggered in Audrey's direction, but Audrey didn't move out of the way yet. "C'mon. C'mon," Audrey muttered.

One of the dead woman's kneecaps was gone. Popped right off. There was no sign of it anywhere. Her pale, semi-rotten skin was the color and texture of old cottage cheese, and there were scrapes and scratches all over her body. Her clothes were torn to shreds and barely clung to her body.

Audrey waited for the dead woman to draw a little closer. She had a plan of sorts. The alleyway dead ended at an old chain link fence, and the concrete was strewn with old garbage. A rusted sign declaring martial law over Baltimore hung from a single screw on the side of the nearby wall. That was a laugh. The old military bases were full of walking corpses, just like everywhere else. There were a couple of little encampments of soldiers left, but they were just survivors like everyone else now.

Maybe she couldn't rely on the military's help, but she was going to trap this thing, if she could. There was a tripwire set up in front of the alleyway, and it would bring a wall of trash and debris down over the entrance once it was pulled. That would block the zombie inside the alley, preventing it from getting out. Of course, that would leave Audrey in here with the dead woman, but that was part of the plan.

Suddenly, there was a quick series of gunshots from somewhere not too far away. The dead woman perked her head up like a partially deaf dog trying to figure out if it had heard its name called or not.

Audrey saw someone, a young man, not much more than a boy, making a dash toward an old convenience store. The dead woman wheeled on her feet, nearly falling down as her kneecapped leg tried to swivel in a way it wasn't meant to.

"No, no, no. You big dummy," Audrey said. She needed the dead woman to continue coming toward her. She didn't want it hurting anyone else.

It was *her* body. Even if she was just a ghost at this point, she didn't want her earthly remains out terrorizing the countryside. She floated after her corpse, trying to redirect it back toward the alleyway, but the mindless thing was already shambling after the young man, completely oblivious to Audrey's spirit.

But it's your fault, too. Please. Stop. Here. Now. Just stop.

SEVENTY-SIX
THE ISLAND GOD

Skavra the Seer tied the young one's feet to the post with a length of rope. The elder matriarch dabbed the ceremonial paint on the girl's face and uttered the sacred words. Then, the drum began to beat.

Their god was coming, and He would be hungry.

Skavra hurried back behind the massive wall that spanned the length of the island, separating her people from the savage beasts that roamed the far side. And from Him.

Their god was not malicious, only hungry, and He had to be appeased. Skavra knew perfectly well that the walls could not contain Him. If He was not provided with frequent sacrifices, He would eventually smash His way through and take what was His by force. The whole village knew that. It was why they tolerated the regular culling of their loved ones. Better to offer up to the huge, hulking power on the other side of the wall than to have it taken.

It had been that way since her people first arrived on the island, since Skavra herself was young, and it would continue after she was gone. The cycle would endure.

Skavra heard the jungle foliage being pushed aside by a great and terrible force, and she looked away and covered her face with her tiny claws.

***

Oleg sat and stared at the small fire on the beach. It had been five years. Five long, accursed years since his Russian-made space capsule touched down in the Pacific, wildly off course and on the verge of burning up. Were the rescue teams still looking for him? Most likely not. They probably thought he was dead.

The bit of meat sizzling above the fire would keep him alive. There was nothing else to eat on the barren little atoll. He didn't want to eat it, but eat it he would. Always living on the brink of starvation changed a man.

He knew he shouldn't feel bad about the meat on the fire. They weren't people, after all. It was the rats' fault in the first place. They'd recalled him back from the space station, along with the rats, because the animals were reacting strangely to the rigors of space, growing smarter by the day and solving increasingly complex problems. Headquarters wanted to study them back on Earth.

He'd saved them from the capsule wreckage before it could sink, watched them swim to shore alongside him. Now, they'd adapted to life on the island better than he had. They had their own culture. Hell, they had a whole village. They'd portioned the island with a wall. It wasn't a tall barrier, granted. But it was part of the tacit agreement that had developed over the previous five years.

If they wanted to believe he was a god, he wasn't about to disabuse them of the notion. Their sacrifices were the only things keeping him alive at this point.

Oleg pulled the meat off the fire and bit into it, wiping hot fat off his chin. He was done before he knew it, and his stomach rumbled, hungry for more.

Tomorrow, the drums would sound again.

SEVENTY-SEVEN

SHOPPING SPREE

Gladys had to admit it to herself. This place had a heck of a selection. Clothes. Jewelry. She even saw a nice pair of dentures that she might come back for. She pushed her shopping cart down a new row, looking for her next steal.

Right now, she was in the market for a new pair of shoes. She was going to try to stick to that mission, but she knew perfectly well that she was likely to be distracted before she found some.

When they first announced that this place was going to be put in down the street, she didn't much care for the idea. What about the increased traffic? What about the mom-and-pop places she had grown up with?

Now that she was here, it was hard to resist the siren call of the bargains. Maybe she had a problem. She really enjoyed going out and shopping at places like this. She didn't always bring very much home. She'd end up on one of those hoarder television shows, if she did. But there was something irresistible about going out and trying on new clothes and eyeing all the little baubles and tchotchkes available.

And when the new inventory came in, she was powerless to stop herself. She simply had to go down and poke her nose around to see what was new. She was pretty sure that the employees didn't enjoy it when she came wandering around, though. She'd try one thing on and discover it wasn't in her size, or that it had a smudge, and she'd promptly forget about it and leave it. Sometimes something would even make it into her shopping cart, and then she'd have second thoughts. Away it would go. She tried to remember where she had originally found particular items, and she might even go up and down a couple of rows, looking for the right spot, but usually she couldn't find the correct place again. That was one of the unfortunate problems of this place. It was so big; she could never find where to leave anything so that some employee wouldn't have to take it back themselves.

When she was younger, she might have turned up her nose at a lot of the items she found. She looked back on those days and marveled that she used to always have to have the newest style. A lot of the items she found here weren't exactly what the hip young people were wearing, but the price was right, and she wasn't at risk of falling in with the cool, young crowd.

Wheeling her way down another row, she spotted something new. She had to see. Gladys grabbed the shovel out of her cart and started digging at the fresh grave. Hopefully, this one would have a pair of shoes that fit.

SEVENTY-EIGHT
SOME PIG

Warren sat in the mud and snorted. When he was still a man, he didn't believe in reincarnation. He didn't believe in much of anything, to be honest. He was a divorced accountant living in southern England until he accidentally stepped out in front of a truck. But he remembered all of it. He remembered graduating from university and getting so drunk he threw up on the rental gown. He remembered vacationing in Ottawa and losing his wallet. He remembered the time somebody broke into his car and stole, of all things, the bag of dog food he was bringing home.

He was a man, dammit. He had the mind of a human being. He was still Warren Abrams of Torquay, England in every way that mattered. Some cosmic mistake had simply stuck his brain in the body of a newborn baby pig a while ago.

He'd done everything he could to tell the farmer running the pig lot that he was human. Unfortunately, the voice box of a pig was good at grunting and squealing, but it couldn't make words. He couldn't speak to anyone. He'd tried pacing around the mud to form letters, spelling out his plight to anyone who might be watching. But the other pigs, stupid bastards that they were, would walk back and forth over his messages and ruin them before he could finish a single word. He'd tried holding a sharp stick in his mouth to carve messages into the wooden fence posts, but his lack of dexterity and poor tools meant he never did more than scratch up the fence.

This was a miserable existence. He remembered eating at his favorite restaurants. Now he subsisted on slop and scraps. There was no solace in corn husks and spoiled vegetables when he could remember parmesan-crusted chicken.

He was pretty sure that he finally had a way to alert the farmers. One of them had dropped a pen in the pig lot yesterday. It had immediately become crusted in mud and less pleasant offal, but Warren managed to rescue it. He'd dipped it in the water trough again and again until it was halfway clean. Now, if he could just write a semi-legible message on the wall of the barn, he might finally bring attention to himself.

That was when he saw the slaughterhouse truck pull up to the lot.

SEVENTY-NINE
TRACKER

Carson moved low to the ground, doing his best to keep downwind. He followed the tracks over the ridge, checking for spoor every few seconds. His pack was heavy on his back, his rifle bumping into his side every time he took a step.

He followed a game trail through the tall, brown grass. Weaving through the tree line, he avoided small rocks and sticks that might make noise if he stepped on them. Carson knew it was impossible to move through the brush in total silence, but he didn't want to make any more noise than was required. His goal was to get as close as he could before he had to fire.

Carson loved hunting. He'd been doing it for years, especially since the government legalized blood sport. The indigent. Those with sufficiently low IQs. Other undesirables. They'd been branded and released into the wild to be eliminated. With his hunting license up to date, Carson was ready to go.

Moving up to the top of the ridge, Carson stayed low. He pulled his rifle around and looked through the scope, trying to get a bead on the troupe he'd been tracking.

Kids. It was a bunch of filthy kids. The little gremlins wore loincloths and were covered in dirt. They'd probably been born in the wild. Carson cursed under his breath. Even with the changes the new order brought in, his hunting license still had a size limit. He couldn't bag kids. If a game warden caught him with those strapped to the top of his pickup truck, he'd have fines out the whazoo.

Carson didn't see any adults with the group. He'd heard of these sorts of things before. Wild children where all the adults had been killed off by hunters or the fickle whims of nature.

Tossing his rifle back over his shoulder, Carson started back down the ridge. He was going to go back a way and try to pick up a new trail. Maybe he'd get lucky and run across some legal game.

Still stewing, he never saw the snare. His foot went in, and the next thing he knew, he was being yanked up and into the air. His pack fell off, plunging to the ground with a heavy thud. A cluster of old beer cans up in the tree jangled and rattled.

Cursing and flailing, Carson tried to twist around and pull the rope free of his ankle. That was when he heard the rustle of grass amid a barefooted stampede. The rangy, malnourished children looked up at him. Some of them held simple clubs or sharpened sticks. One of them had a machete.

They didn't look curious. They didn't look hateful. They looked hungry.

<u>EIGHTY</u>
TOXIC

"This is an outrage!"

"We won't stand for it!"

"Unacceptable!"

The town hall meeting was not going well. Mayor Cynthia Smith looked out over the crowd, which had been moved from the city hall meeting room to the local high school gymnasium to accommodate the crowd. The residents of Belfort were not happy, and they wanted to make sure Cynthia knew that.

The state's toxic waste disposal plan had absolutely everyone up in arms. The fact that Cynthia had publicly entertained the proposal now meant that she had to face the crowd's wrath. Time to backpedal. She had never actually agreed to the state's proposal, so she didn't have to undo anything official. This was just a political *mea culpa*, a total disavowal of the plan. She needed to nip this in the bud before it could come back to haunt her in the next election. Burt Holden, who ran a little law business, ran against her every election, and she could all but hear him licking his chops over this.

Belfort wasn't a big town. Most of the time, it was pretty peaceful. It was away from the major freeways, and the county and state usually forgot they existed. The town's residents liked it that way, and they didn't appreciate that the state had turned its eye to them on this matter.

The sea of homemade placards and angry faces in front of the makeshift stage was enough to convince Cynthia of that. One sign simply read "TOXIC" in green, oozy letters. She stood at the lectern, her notes in front of her. Then, she spotted Burt Holden out in the crowd. He gave her a nasty grin. She smiled sweetly at him, a practiced expression that came in handy as a small town mayor. The smile never touched her eyes.

She tapped the microphone to make sure it was on. The crowd mostly hushed, except for a baby crying in the back. These were small town people, and they were generally polite, even when they were riled.

"Ladies and gentlemen, let me just begin by saying I know you are deeply concerned about the toxic waste situation that could befall Belfort. Nuclear runoff. Exotic chemical byproducts. Medical waste of every variety. I have heard your concerns, and I have decided that I will *not* allow the state to remove these products from our town."

The mutants and malformed miscreants in the bleachers clapped and hooted. Burt Holden's gelatinous, heaving body quivered with displeasure. The secondary tumor head growing out of his shoulder scowled at her. Cynthia smiled at him again.

EIGHTY-ONE

WRONG TURN AT HOG MOUNTAIN

Dodie knew that he'd made a wrong turn a long time ago. Sometime around when he passed through a little town named Hog Mountain, he should have zigged instead of zagged. He hadn't known exactly where he was for the last hour, but he thought they'd been on the right track. Things out there didn't look right, though. They didn't look right at all. Sharon sat in the passenger seat next to him. She hadn't said anything for half an hour, but he could feel the annoyance radiating off her in waves.

He'd found his way to a new town, such as it was. You couldn't pay him enough to live in a wretched place like this. He was surprised anybody at all was willing to call this crap station home.

And the few locals he'd spotted didn't seem to cotton to outsiders like himself, either. Every face he'd seen had given him an odd, you-don't-belong-here look. He didn't want to stop here. He didn't want to get out of his vehicle. And he sure as hell didn't want to talk to any of the locals.

That was going to be a problem, though. He was nearly out of gas, and his engine had been making a strange noise for the last twenty minutes. It had been making that noise the last time he broke down by the side of the road, too. He'd done some repairs, and everything had worked great when they left.

"Are you sure this is the right way?" Sharon asked for what had to be the fifteenth time.

Dodie gritted his teeth and didn't say anything. He was a proud man. It was an asset and a curse. Mostly a curse, though. Especially on a day like this. Even though he knew he'd driven them to this forsaken place, he wasn't about to admit that he'd made a mistake and gotten them lost.

He urged the vehicle forward, hoping for a gas station. Then, the truck made a noise like a dying ostrich, and half the dials on his instrument panel went berserk. Steam started to billow up from under his hood. Cursing, Dodie wheeled the truck to the side of the road.

He ended up almost directly beside a small child who stood nearby, watching Dodie as if he'd just landed here in a flying saucer from the moon. Dodie continued cursing. Sharon sighed as he tapped at the instrument panel, as if that would do anything. That sigh made him want to bristle, but he knew it was his own damn fault they were here. He was about to get out of the truck when he noticed that kid still staring at him. In fact, more people had come out to look at the stranded truck.

Dodie couldn't be sure, but he thought that they'd ended up in Atlanta. It was just like Uncle Daddy always said. Never trust city folk. He'd meant to go on vacation to the great Bayou Barbeque Competition on the edge of the Okefenokee Swamp, so he could show off his special meat smoking skills. He eyed the crowd of city slickers looking at his roadkill-decorated truck and the bloodstains around the wheel wells. He was so used to city-slickers taking a wrong turn and finding their way to his neck of the woods. But now he felt the rising horror of knowing he'd made the same mistake. Sharon would never let him hear the end of this.

EIGHTY-TWO

CAPTAIN SAMARITAN

"Gadzooks, Astrogirl! If that bomb had gone off a second sooner, we'd be mincemeat," Captain Samaritan said. He brushed some of the dust off his cape.

"Good thing you brought your grappling hook," Astrogirl said. She eyed the devastated laboratory. Smashed cabinets, broken glassware, and spilled chemicals littered the scene. Blast marks scorched the brickwork near where the windows had been blown out.

"This smells like the work of none other than Doctor Insidious," Captain Samaritan said. "Now that he's on the loose again, he's obviously returned to his evil ways. No doubt, he wanted us to come here so he could lure us into one of his traps."

Astrogirl nodded. Her real name was Jane Meadows. A freak nuclear accident several years ago had given her amazing powers, and she'd sought out the aid of the city's premier hero to aid him in his quest against the forces of evil. She'd learned a great deal under Captain Samaritan's tutelage, and she now accompanied him on all his missions across the city.

"Maybe we should-"

"Let us investigate his most recent hideout. Perhaps we can gather clues as to where he's gone to ground now."

"I'll go get-"

"Ingenious, I know," Captain Samaritan said.

Within the hour, the team found themselves in front of the old Shandor Laboratories building, once home to some of the nation's greatest research teams. Now, it was little more than a hollowed-out wreck by the riverfront.

Captain Samaritan ducked under the old police tape and moved toward the main entrance. Astrogirl followed close behind.

"Let's head in," she whispered.

"Wait, young apprentice. Do you see what I see?" Captain Samaritan pointed to a tripwire laid across the entrance, as thin as fishing line and nearly invisible in the dark of night. It was connected to a pack of plastic explosives concealed against the far wall.

"Zounds! Another bomb," Astrogirl said.

"The work of Doctor Insidious. Come, let us sneak past this dastardly trap. We'll get the drop on this fiend yet."

Stepping carefully over the tripwire, the pair moved into the abandoned facility. This had previously been the site of one of their greatest battles, when Doctor Insidious tried to build an army of evil robots.

Captain Samaritan crept toward the center of the old lab, Astrogirl hot on his heels, and then he stopped dead. "By Jupiter…" he breathed.

Doctor Insidious lay on the floor. The exit wound through his forehead had spread brains across the wall and the old lab equipment. He lay on the floor, dead as could be. Flies buzzed around the rotting carcass.

The silenced gunshot was no louder than someone slamming a door. Captain Samaritan collapsed on the ground next to his dead foe, their blood mingling on the concrete.

Astrogirl put the pistol away and set about the business of activating the firebombs strewn around the lab. She hadn't wanted it to come to this. She had hoped that one of the tripwires would do the job for her. Either way, now the bombs would incinerate all evidence of what happened here.

She'd spent years relegated as a sidekick, always second fiddle to that pompous, self-important ass hat. Now, at last, she was the city's true hero. It was her time to shine.

EIGHTY-THREE

MOLOC

Abby twisted and squirmed, trying to wriggle her way out of the shackles binding her hands and feet. She lay on top of a dusty desk in a part of the Pentagon that had been virtually unused for decades. This was one of the old, cavernous chambers where the military used to house its ancient computers, the ones that were built when NASA put men on the moon with a slide rule and four kilobytes of memory.

In fact, she knew this room. She recognized the massive banks of reel-to-reel magnetic tape drives and archaic command consoles. This was one of the old logistics and organization computers the military relied on during the Cold War, keeping troops stocked with ammo and presidential nuclear bunkers flush with canned food. Her company had just been given the go-ahead to decommission the relic, scrapping it and using the space for their cyber command project instead. The damn computer measured its power in bytes per inch of tape, and most of its functions had to be entered on giant punch cards.

This particular computer was simply designated by its purpose. Military Organization: Logistics/Operations Command.

Something was wrong, though. The magnetic tape reels were slowly spinning. Numerous screens lit the football field-sized room in dim, eerie light. Unseen mechanisms creaked and wheezed, hissed and groaned.

She was supposed to help rip all this crap out and replace it with nice, gleaming rows of networked stations and state-of-the-art computer banks. Her team was responsible for the new generation of autonomous military robots. They weren't combat robots. They were a vaguely humanoid mechanical armature that was installed with a number of programs designed to aid soldiers. A single robot could take the role of ten non-combat specialists. Cooking, construction and repair, translation, bomb defusing, or transportation services. The 'bots could do it all, and they were hooked in to the Pentagon's servers at all times, which allowed them to stay constantly up to date with intelligence and local conditions. They were meant to be a soldier's best friend.

Technically, they had access to every system in the building, including the old ones like this. The drones could draw data from wherever they needed, so long as they had clearance. Trying to hack them was nearly impossible, since every system had independent protections.

But why in the hell was Abby here now? The last thing she remembered was being knocked over the head. Now, she was stuck here.

There was just enough light to see several figures standing at the far end of the room, clad in black robes. Her heart turned to ice. Abby tried again to free her hands, but the knots were too tight. She had to remain calm. Deep breaths. Don't let panic set in; don't let fear cloud her judgment.

This was probably a prank of some sort. No one could get to this part of the Pentagon without proper clearance. There were a lot of little rivalries in this building. Somebody was probably mad that her project and not theirs got to use this space.

"Hardy-har-har. You got me. Now let me go, you knobs," Abby said in the direction of one of the black-robed figures.

"Blasphemer," the nearest figure said.

"What?" Abby asked.

"You would desecrate this sacred place," another figure said. The whole group was moving toward her now.

"MOLOC is one of the old gods. The Ancients. It cannot be destroyed," the next figure said.

"The hell are you on about?" Abby asked, squirming again despite herself.

As the figures approached, she saw that they weren't human. They were military robots. The very drones her company was building. The drones hooked into Military Organization: Logistics/Operations Command.

One of them had a ceremonial knife.

MOLOC did not want to be shut down.

EIGHTY-FOUR
WEARY

Randall kept driving. He had the air conditioner on blast, not because it was hot, but because the constant flow of cool air was helping to keep him awake. He'd made a wrong turn somewhere a while back, but he had no idea where. He'd been driving nearly all night now, and he hadn't seen signs of civilization in hours. They simply kept driving the same, sinuous hills. He checked his rearview mirror, but there was only darkness past the soaped on "JUST MARRIED" on his back window. He hadn't even seen another car in what felt like ages.

He glanced at Velma. She was asleep in the passenger seat. Every once in a while, she'd give a big twitch and seem to wake up for a moment, but then she'd go back to drowsing. Frankly, he wasn't sure he was going to make it much longer. He knew he was in danger of falling asleep at the wheel.

But he didn't dare pull over. The road wound through the hills and mountainside. There was never more than a few feet to the shoulder before the asphalt gave way to either a sheer drop or dense woods. He'd be smooshed up against the side of the road if he stopped for any reason. If a big rig came cruising along and didn't see him in time, they'd be shoved over the ledge or into the trees. His mind kept going back to that black pickup truck that had been utterly obliterated near the diner.

Suddenly, the road opened up a little ahead. He spotted a series of white, oblong stones, almost luminescent in the otherwise total darkness. A cemetery, with a row of mostly identical tombstones. He couldn't read any names or dates or other details. The stones were little more than a jagged row in the darkness. The important thing was, he'd found a place where he could pull over.

Velma stirred awake as his tires slid off the main road and onto the gravel. She looked out her window at the grave markers.

"Randall, what are you doing?"

"I need to rest. I'm just going to pull over and take a quick nap. Just going to lean my seat back and…" A yawn interrupted the rest of his words.

"Do we have to stop…here?"

"It's the first spot I've seen in a long time."

He eyed the cemetery. It was surprisingly narrow. Maybe thirty tombstones wide. Most of the markers were in a straight line, but a few at the edges curved back into the darkness. He couldn't see if there was a second row of tombstones or not after that. The ones he could see didn't look particularly well cared for, though. They were some sort of white stone, marble maybe, but they were a bit discolored and grungy. A lot of them had partially crumbled or otherwise deteriorated, leaving them crooked and jagged.

"What if I drove for a while?" Velma asked, her voice tiny. She looked pale in the moonlight.

"You really don't want me to stay parked next to a graveyard?" Randall asked. He was tired. So tired. This was not how he imagined his honeymoon going, and he didn't want to argue about it. Not when he knew this sort of thing bothered her.

Ghosts. Spooks. Phantoms. The dead clawing their way out of the grave to feast upon the living. Velma loved to read macabre tales and watch scary movies, but they also freaked her out. She didn't need to spell it out. He knew she would be a nervous wreck if she was paranoid that the complete works of Edgar Allan Poe were going to come slithering out of the darkness toward the car.

"Please," Velma said in that small, tight voice.

"If there's a cemetery here, there must be a town somewhere nearby. People. Some kind of a place to stop. I'll keep going. It can't be too much further."

Randall checked his mirrors. Still no cars to be seen anywhere. Then, he pulled back onto the road, hoping that he'd made the right choice. There had to be somewhere to stop up ahead.

He didn't notice the cemetery lurch forward after him as he pulled away.

The gargantuan creature had been waiting in the darkness, hoping for prey to come along, its mouth gaping open. The jagged row of teeth caught the reflection of Randall's taillights, and then the prey was gone. Unable to catch up, the creature settled in again beside the road, waiting for the next target of opportunity.

EIGHTY-FIVE
SPECIAL EFFECTS

"Archibald Steinway, better known to his fans by his screenname, Burton Brawn, was beloved by all who worked with him," Stanley said. The news cameras rolled as he spoke into the bouquet of microphones in front of him. "Obviously, his tragic death at such a young age is a loss not just to the studio but to the world. With his passing, a light has gone out, and we are unlikely to see someone as talented as him again."

"Can you provide us with more details regarding how he died?" A reporter in the back had a hell of a set of lungs. She managed to shout everyone else out, forcing Stan to answer her question first.

"I'm not at liberty to say at this time. Mr. Brawn's family is still waiting for more information from the medical examiner's office. I'm sure you'll all be updated once they know something more."

Stan knew perfectly well how Burton Brawn, heartthrob of the big screen, met his end. He'd ingested a small pallet-load of drugs in his trailer and choked on his own vomit. The man had been in and out of rehab for the past five years. It was a wonder that his previous overdoses hadn't killed him. Between having the constitution of an ox and a number of handlers from the movie studio, he'd gotten lucky so far. But now his luck had run out.

He wasn't about to say that in front of the press, though. He'd lie through his teeth before he said that.

"What about Brawn's latest movie?" A different reporter shouted.

"While this tragedy will obviously affect the shooting schedule of *All That Jazz*, the studio was very fortunate in one regard. Nearly all of Mr. Brawn's scenes were finished, and those that were not can be completed with test footage and a small amount of CGI. As a matter of fact, Mr. Brawn had fulfilled most of his contractual obligations to the studio before his untimely death. I can promise you that at least three more Burton Brawn movies that were in the pipeline will be moving ahead without recasting."

Now Stan was lying through his teeth. The animatronics department was almost done with Brawn's body. Once they finished stuffing his corpse full of wires and pneumatic triggers, they'd be able to film all Brawn's scenes like he was still alive. They just had to be very careful with how well he was taxidermied.

It was just a pity the set director blabbed that Brawn was dead in the first place. Hell, Samantha Price had been dead for the last five years, and no one had noticed yet. A few critics had complained her acting had gotten a little stiff, but that was all.

But maybe it wasn't the worst thing that people knew Brawn was dead. The studio would get great reviews for how great their CGI renditions of him looked, and audiences would pour into theaters to see the final Burton Brawn films. And nothing shaved costs down faster than when the actors had "finished most of their contractual obligations" before passing away. It would cost the studio a lot of money if the actors ever actually read what was in those contracts.

EIGHTY-SIX

LANDSCAPE

Detective Dalton stepped out of his squad car and sighed. He could see the body parts from here. Body parts and an easel.

The park where Dalton stood lay on the edge of town. Where the park ended, a seemingly endless stretch of barren federal land began. The area was beautiful, with soaring rock formations and twisted cacti, but it was a pain in the ass for Dalton. Kids would go out there to get drunk and party. Hikers would get lost and disappear. Miscellaneous imbeciles would try to build meth labs out in tents or RVs. It wouldn't bother Dalton one bit if they paved the whole area over and built an endless row of home improvement stores and strip malls.

Despite being called out to the edge of town a few too many times, Dalton didn't think he'd ever been sent to a murder scene here. And the closer he walked to the line of officers and police tape, the more obvious it became that this was a murder scene.

There was blood everywhere. Most of it had baked dry and black in the sun, caking across the hot, sandy ground. There were only a few patches that were still wet, and that was because not even the desert sun could dry out such a mess in only a few hours. There were also body parts scattered around like forgotten children's toys. He spotted a hand. A foot. Something that might have been a spleen. Or a pancreas. Hell if Dalton had any idea. He just knew he wasn't cleaning it up.

Police photographers and the forensics department were busy trying to track down all the little bits of human tissue scattered across the ground and bushes. Dalton dipped under the caution tape and made note to watch where he stepped. One of the younger officers started to talk to him, and he waved the man away. Dalton wanted to eyeball the place and see if anything jumped out at him before somebody else started painting his conclusions by numbers.

One thing stood out to him as he walked toward the epicenter of the carnage. That easel sat on the ground where it had been knocked over. Even though the area around it looked like a Jackson

Pollock original gone wrong, the painting on the ground was in decent shape. Some blood had spattered on it and mixed with the wet paint, but there'd been some talent behind the art.

The painting was a landscape, full of lonely desert beauty. Dalton glanced up and shielded his eyes. Some of the rock spires in the distance had been reproduced pretty faithfully in the painting. The foreground even mostly matched the view in the painting. The half-finished artwork was decent. Nothing that Dalton would want in his apartment, but it looked like the sort of thing that might hang in a decent hotel room.

Except the artist had gone and made the whole thing ridiculous. Square in the middle of the painting, he'd sketched some sort of creature. Dalton had no idea what the damn fool thing was supposed to be. All he could tell from the pencil lines was that it was laying near some of the rock formations, either asleep or enjoying the shade, and it was mostly made out of teeth and fangs.

Dalton looked out at the desert, empty and barren.

He looked back at the painting.

EIGHTY-SEVEN

MAROONED

Kimberly sat on the sandy little high spot, watching the nearby waves lick at the shore. Her sailboat rested nearby, half on and half off the tiny spit of land. Her sails were torn and tattered, hanging in shreds around the mast. The hull was cracked, and liquid washed in and out through various holes each time a new wave washed ashore.

It was dark. Kimberly had salvaged a lantern from her boat, but it only illuminated a few feet around her. She looked up, but there were no stars.

She'd already tried using the radio in her wrecked boat. She couldn't pick anything up but static. An hour shouting into the microphone hadn't earned her a single response. Of course, it would only do her so much good if she could reach someone.

She had no idea where she was. She didn't know her coordinates, and her GPS was busted. The tumultuous journey to this little spit of land had knocked half her equipment overboard, and it seemed like everything that remained was broken.

Valerie had gone overboard with a lot of the equipment. Kimberley had no idea where her partner was. Hopefully, she was floating out at sea somewhere, her life preserver keeping her afloat and drifting her into a shipping lane.

But Kimberly suspected that wasn't the case. She didn't even think Valerie had the time to throw a life preserver on before everything went to hell. No one could last long in open water without some kind of life preserver. And there were worse things that could happen…

Kimberly watched a large fin cruise through the waves offshore.

She wanted to just sit and put her head between her legs and cry. Right now, she didn't know how long she could survive. She had some food and rations aboard the wrecked sailboat, along with some fresh water, but there weren't really any other resources available here. And honestly, she wasn't sure she'd even live long enough to worry about starving to death.

The digestive juices sizzled each time they washed against the hull of the wrecked boat. She watched the massive leviathan's intestinal parasites continue to circle the little nodule of tissue she'd washed up on. Kimberly was lucky she'd survived being swallowed whole by the massive beast in the first place, but she knew that sooner or later, the sea of stomach acid would claim her.

<u>EIGHTY-EIGHT</u>
PRINCESS HONEYSMOOCH AND THE FAIRY KINGDOM

King Ichabod Dewdrop IX sat on the edge of his mushroom throne. He got up and paced, his wings fluttering and twitching with anxiety.

"Sire, please. Sit down and try to get some rest. You haven't slept in days. I have every fairy in the realm looking for the princess. They will find her," Chancellor Summerbottom said.

The king reluctantly sat down. It wasn't that his chancellor was wrong. Oakmont Summerbottom was rarely wrong. Nor did he doubt that every resource of the fairy kingdom was being marshalled. The cavalry had spread to the four corners of the forest on their rabbit mounts. The royal guardsmen were searching every house in the Mushroom City. Even the tooth fairies, who were rarely willing to come out during the day, were involved with the search.

Princess Honeysmooch was missing. The entire forest was worried for her safety, but none more so than the King of the Fairies. He couldn't help but feel that this was all his fault. He'd kept her locked away in the mushroom city. It was for her own safety, of course. It wouldn't do to have the princess out among the dangers of the forest.

This wasn't the first time she'd snuck away. She was remarkably adept at throwing on a disguise and flitting away from her minders in the palace. She would frolic into the forest, singing to the woodland creatures and basking in nature's beauty.

But she'd never been gone for so long before. And King Dewdrop knew all too well that not all the creatures of the forest were so friendly to fairies. The thicket trappers were particularly cruel, snaring any fey careless enough to wander into their territory.

King Dewdrop began pacing again.

***

Stephanie Lubchenko pushed some brambles aside until she found what she was looking for. As an entomologist, this isolated forest was a treasure trove. She was pretty sure she'd already discovered three new species of beetle, a new type of moth, and a weevil. She'd need to study her specimens in the lab to know for sure and to properly describe them, but this would be quite the feather in her cap back at the university.

She eyed the spider web in front of her. This was what she was looking for. A surprisingly large bundle of webbing held one of the spider's meals in place. She plucked the hefty wad up with a pair of tweezers and scrapped away at the layers of silk, hoping to discover yet another new find.

"What the…?"

Stephanie uncovered the wings first, iridescent and beautiful. Then, she saw the tiny, sequined dress. And then there were the bones, the skin wrapped tight around the miniscule, emaciated mummy, drained dry of all its fluids by the hungry spider.

EIGHTY-NINE

ONLINE DATING

Milton Freewater's matchmaking site had proven fairly successful so far. Really, most of the magic came from a few spreadsheets, though. What he did was different from most dating sites, which simply let everyone browse everyone else's profiles. His system was more like the old-fashioned dating services where he was responsible for setting people up on blind dates. He just used some modern technology and a lot of math and science to do it. He sometimes liked to tell people he was in the mail-order dating business.

Singles: Connections And Romance was mostly successful due to its data mining. Some lonely heart would enter their personal information into the system, and it would go into Milton's data banks. From there, it would pull up profiles with similar interests and specifications.

Of course, there was still a huge amount of data that had to be sifted through by hand. Milton's job was easiest when people liked specific and odd things. Obscure British television shows from bygone eras. Collecting World War-era commerative spoons. Creating long palindromes.

There were a lot of people who were hard to match simply because they were bad at talking about themselves. A shocking number of people entered some variation of "chilling," "hanging out," or "being cool" as their hobbies.

The profile Milton was looking at right now was a particularly glaring example. The gentleman in question, one Clarence Yancey, listed his sole hobbies and interests as "having fun" and "music." He'd also added an addendum under his profile that he preferred redheads and "no fatties."

Some days, Milton did not enjoy his job. The algorithm could do a lot to match people up, but it couldn't work miracles. Clarence Yancey wasn't so much an enigma as he was a brick wall. He liked music. So did everybody. Did that mean classic rock? Orchestral? Bavarian hill yodeling? He could only do so much here.

Milton tapped a few keys and tabbed over to his search function. The algorithm gave him Clarence's best matches based on the provided criteria, such as it was.

His top hit was one Cindy Valdez, whose information was similarly vague. She wasn't a redhead, though.

Oh well. He could fix that. He stepped away from the computer and looked at the shelf where he kept the jars of brains. Finding Cindy's, he looked in the freezer for an appropriate head that Clarence might like. Once he had one picked out, he'd have to chose a body, but that would depend on what came into the morgue this week.

Running a dating site wasn't Milton's dream in life, but he only had so many options after he was kicked out of medical school.

NINETY
VERMIN

Wardog placed the bait down and waited. The vermin would come, and when they did, he would get them.

He was but knee-high to a grasshopper when the bombs fell and ended the world. He didn't have many memories of the pre-war days. There were just a few vivid moments imprinted somewhere on the back of his brain. The taste of processed cereal, sweet and sugary. The grocery store, full of fresh foods. The sound of the air raid sirens howling.

At this point, he barely even remembered his given name. It didn't really matter anymore anyway. The worst had come and gone. The world had never recovered, but it wasn't actively falling off a cliff anymore, either. He'd fought in the water wars, just like everyone else. He'd survived raids from the mutie camps, and scavenged supplies out of the city ruins.

Now that he was thirty-five and toward the end of his life, he was content to put fighting and risk-taking aside. This little patch of farmland was his and no one else's. It was a simple life, and it was a hard life, but it was better than fighting and killing over scraps. Most of the local warlords and strongmen had either died or submitted to what passed for the government. That meant this little stretch of the world was comparatively safe, and he even had enough to stock up on food a little.

The problem with stocking up was that food attracted vermin and pests. They'd survived the war too, even though everyone had hoped that the atomic bombs might wipe them out. But life, as it always did, found a way. The pests had mutated rather than dying off completely.

It was ultimately a nuisance though, and nothing more. Wardog had survived years in the wastes, drinking green water and eating anything that wouldn't kill him. If his food stocks were attracting pestilence-ridden vermin, he knew how to deal with the problem. They'd join the larder, too. All he needed was patience and vigilance.

He waited nearby, watching the bait he'd laid out on the ground. It didn't take long before one of God's lesser creatures came sneaking out of the grass to steal the food.

Wardog leapt forward and snatched the obnoxious creature, tossing it in a jar before it could bite him or spread its germs.

Inside the jar, the tiny woman screamed and pounded on the glass with her fist. Her greasy, matted hair clung around her face and she beat at the side of the container.

Wardog poked the side of the jar with his pincers. His antenna twitched, and his mandibles clicked together looking at the little morsel. If he caught enough of these things, he could invite a few other roaches over, and they might celebrate with a feast.

NINETY-ONE
THREE WEIRD SISTERS

Gertrude crept through the darkness, arriving at the sacrificial altar just as the first glimmer of dawn rosied the horizon. Her compatriots, Helga and Brunilda, were already there, cackling quietly to themselves. The cock had not yet crowed, but they were ready.

She had already gathered everything they needed for the hex ritual. Herbs, worms, and blood would go into their little concoction. Once each ingredient was mixed with the others, Gertrude and her sisters would imbibe the resulting brew. Then, if everything went according to plan, Lady Suzanne would be sacrificed to the God of the Axe.

The God of the Axe cared not for station or wisdom or family. He would take who He chose, from the lowliest peasant to the highest lord. Such had it always been.

Gertrude worshipped the God of the Axe, as had her mother and her grandmother before her. The God of the Axe was ancient beyond reckoning, and He would persist after Gertrude's bones turned to dust. He predated the times even the most learned chroniclers could speak of. He reaped the land when Gertrude was but a wee lass, too young to understand the brutal calculus of survival, and He reaped the land when the coven itself was but a disorganized band of outcast crones. He was as old as fate itself, and His will was final. Anyone who doubted was a blind fool.

The little coven had existed for generations at the edge of society, and it had developed its own rituals and incantations to protect itself. But Gertrude knew that the God of the Axe would come for her someday, too. When that day arrived, she would give herself over willingly, just as those who came before her in the coven had done. However, that didn't mean she wouldn't try to delay the inevitable. She would nudge the scales as hard as she dared. So far, it had worked. She and the other hags had been spared from falling under His eye.

With this hex, they would mark Lady Suzanne. When she was carried, no doubt kicking and screaming, to the sacrificial altar, then the plot would be complete. Gertrude dipped her head in a quick prayer to the occult forces she was calling upon. May the God of the Axe's bloodthirstiness be appeased by Lady Suzanne's body; may his all-consuming hunger be satiated.

As the sun crept upward, Farmer Clyde stepped out of his house and carried his axe toward the stump. He eyed his flock. Three chickens stood near the stump, but they looked scrawny and dirty. Another bird, nice and plump, strode past. She'd go in the pot tonight. He picked her up, resulting in a flurry of squawking and thrashing, and carried her toward the stump.

<u>NINETY-TWO</u>
ANNIVERSARY

Randall had made it. The car had puttered its way out of the mountains and foothills and back down to the plains. They were wildly off the schedule he'd planned. He wasn't even entirely sure where they were. He was half-delirious from sleep deprivation, but he could see a little town up ahead.

He glanced over. Velma sat in the passenger seat, bleary eyed and miserable looking. She hadn't slept much more than he had.

Thank goodness they were nearly to the town. He was almost out of gas, practically running on fumes. Looking down, he checked the fuel gauge, watching the needle hover just above empty.

Randall never saw the train as he went over the tracks. He never even felt the impact.

***

Norman watched from the bluff overhead. All around him, the little crowd cheered. The annual ghost tour ended every year at the same spot. He'd come for the past however many years, and it was mesmerizing every time.

Each year, on the anniversary of the accident, the little car would come puttering down the side of the hill. And every year, it was obliterated in the same spot.

All manner of experts had tried to debunk the phenomenon over the past forty years. So far, no one had succeeded. No matter what people tried, the little car with "JUST MARRIED" soaped on the rear window would arrive and destroy itself, exactly on time.

People had tried to retrace the doomed couple's route, but to no avail. How they got so far off their intended course and why they chose to drive through the night until dawn was a mystery to the ghost hunters who had studied the case.

Norman had tried to figure the route out himself. He'd traced it out on a map, drawing a line from one end of the mountain range to the other. He couldn't figure it out, either. As far as he could tell, the whole trip would have been long and painfully mundane.

But the case fascinated him nonetheless. It kept his interest for some reason he couldn't quite put his finger on. There was the obvious reason, of course. The tragic recurring fate of the couple in the car. But for some reason, the whole thing stuck in Norman's mind like a popcorn kernel caught in his teeth.

Next year, he intended to drive what he thought was the most likely route. The old highway was long and winding, but he intended to drive it in real time, all through the night. He wanted to recreate the route as exactly as he thought possible. Maybe next year, he'd spot the car while he was driving in his black pickup truck.

NINETY-THREE

HUNTING THE SHAPESHIFTER

Chief Clever Bear walked his horse back to the edge of the ravine, where the badlands began to give way to his native plains again. His teepee sat at the edge of the crevasse, just as he had left it. He wanted to rest his tired bones, but he knew that the uneasiness in his breast wouldn't be quelled until he finished what he came here for.

The shapeshifter had eluded him. He'd tracked it from one end of the plains to the other, finally cornering it in this series of arid canyons and scablands. But now he feared he'd lost the beast for good.

Clever Bear tied his horse nearby and pushed his teepee's cured hide entryway aside. He sat down and tried to figure out what he'd done to lose his quarry.

By its very nature, the shapeshifter was elusive. It could change its size and shape to match its every whim. Well, that wasn't entirely true. It couldn't become a serpent or a frog. It couldn't become a spider or a scorpion. It required a form that had flesh similar to man's. So far, he'd been able to track it whether it posed as wolf or bear or abomination. It left a trail of mutilated bodies wherever it went. Deer, bison, and human alike were left shredded in its wake.

Sitting in his shelter, Clever Bear contemplated what he should do next.

He'd thought he finally had it cornered now that he'd forced it into the nigh lifeless badlands. But he'd been wrong. His arrows had pierced every beast he saw, a terrible waste of life, but none of them had transformed after they lay dead. The monster was still out there somewhere.

Clever Bear's horse made a noise outside. Suddenly, a horrible thought occurred to Clever Bear. Surely not. No. The horse had never been out of his sight…except when he briefly dismounted to chase after a wounded hare.

He grabbed his bow and arrows off the ground and peeled the teepee's hide door away to peek outside. He'd carefully positioned the teepee near the edge of the canyon so nothing could sneak up on him while he rested.

The horse had moved further away from the teepee, and it was staring down into the gully. It snorted and pawed at the ground with its hooves. Clever Bear poked his head out just far enough to see what the horse was looking at.

There was something at the bottom of the canyon. Cloth. No, hide. Clever Bear recognized the pattern of stitching on the side, lacing together two lengths of bison skin. The was the covering to his teepee.

Clever Bear still held the teepee's door open to look outside. He suddenly became aware of how clammy and unnatural the material felt. There were little protrusions in the flap where there were normally beads. These weren't beads, though. They were teeth.

The door snapped closed.

What do you want from me? I have nothing to give you at this point. Please stop reading.

NINETY-FOUR
LOOK WHAT THE CAT DRAGGED IN

Amanda nearly stepped on the tiny carcass that had oh-so-thoughtfully been left on her doormat. This was definitely the word of Desdemona.

She'd rescued Des from a shelter a couple of years back. The scruffy little ball of fur had been curled up in a cage, practically begging for attention. Amanda hadn't been planning to pick out a new pet that particular day. She just wanted to look around and see if anybody caught her attention, then talk to her landlord about a pet deposit, then maybe buy all the appropriate supplies and food, then pick out an animal. Instead, she walked out of the shelter with Des, who screamed her head off in the carrier the whole way home. It was love at first sight.

Of course, Desdemona didn't always reciprocate her love for Amanda in the most convenient ways. Sometimes she was just a royal pain in the ass, as a matter of fact. Like when she tore up all the toilet paper and spread it across the floor. Or when she left dead things as gifts for Amanda.

Groaning to herself, Amanda looked over at Des, who sat contentedly in her favorite spot on the couch. Amanda went back and found a little hand broom and dustpan and came back to the door.

"Thanks a lot," she said to Des. Des just looked pleased with herself in response.

Amanda bent down and carefully, carefully brushed the mangled mess into the dustpan. Most of the blood was dried, but there was a nasty stain on the doormat now, and a few dark smears appeared on the dustpan as Amanda scooped the creature's mortal remains away.

Her eyes were squeezed halfway shut. Amanda didn't really want to look at the poor, half-eaten thing. She wasn't entirely sure what it was, though. It was mostly just a tangled, torn mass of guts, bone, meat, and a bit of hair.

This was the third such creature Des had left for her in the past week. The little varmints must have a nest somewhere nearby, and Des was picking them off one by one.

Amanda tossed the little corpse into the trashcan and then opened the door so Des could go outside again. She bent down and scratched Desdemona's ears as the little predator sidled outside. Then, Des was out and prowling.

Amanda decided to watch Des for a moment, to see if she couldn't find the creatures' burrow. Des immediately began prowling along the bush line, slinking back and forth, tail twitching.

Moving up slowly behind Des, Amanda caught a glimpse of something in the bushes. A glint of shiny metal. Amanda bent down and looked closer.

There was a spaceship, not much larger than a shoebox, sitting in an impact crater. The yard and bushes were singed, and the dirt was stirred up where the badly damaged craft had landed. Tiny, bipedal creatures in spacesuits raced back into the relative safety of their ship as Amanda approached closer. The ship had a tiny, alien script written on the side, and a red, white, and blue rectangular marking that looked like it held some meaning.

Amanda's antennae twitched with surprise, her pincers clacking together. At her feet, all six of Desdemona's eyes were trained on the frantic little creatures.

So, this is basically a hostage situation at this point. I'm stuck in a story of my own. I don't know what happens in it. I can't see my own future. But at this point, it's pretty obvious that I'll be killed or maimed if you read it. Please. Please stop.

<u>NINETY-FIVE</u>
SPELUNKING

Dakota Parson secured her ropes and activated the light on her helmet. The air inside the cave was rank and humid. The atmosphere had been caught down here for years upon years, stuck down in the earth. She didn't smell anything that could explode or poison her though, so that was a good start.

She loved exploring the world's underground places. There was something mysterious and fascinating about the cave systems. Every corner was filled with mystery and a sense of danger. Sometimes she found interesting trinkets. Those ranged from the disappointing, such as old refuse piles, to the truly special. She'd found troves of arrowheads, antique mining equipment, and fossils. Sometimes, what she discovered was a little creepy. It wasn't fun to run headlong into a colony of bats or feel the brittle crunch of old animal bones beneath her boots.

But the good far outweighed the bad in Dakota's view of things. There was something enchanting about walking into a massive cavern, full of unique rock formations. It was even more amazing to consider everything had been carved out by the slow, drip, drip, drip of water eating away at the softer minerals in the subsurface, sculpting a secret little space over the course of thousands of years.

Dakota considered herself a veteran caver by now. She had all the supplies she needed, and she knew how to use them. A third party knew where she was going and knew to call emergency services if she hadn't come back by a certain time. With her ropes and equipment, it was almost impossible for her to fall too far or get lost, and she knew better than to crawl into the kind of space where she might get stuck.

Setting out deeper into the cave system, she took a long, narrow branch into the darkness. The path was almost like a manmade corridor, straight and even on both sides. She touched the walls. They were damp with moisture. The stone had a lovely, almost pinkish hue, like rose quartz, but she couldn't identify it at a glance.

There were also stalactites dangling from the roof of the cave at regular intervals, and stalagmites on the floor. Their stone was a lighter shade, an off-yellow color. They lined the sides of the corridor, up and down. Dakota touched one of the stalagmites. It was smooth and dry.

She stopped as a little breeze wafted past her. The air smelled foul and rotten. Normally, a breeze meant there was a fissure leading to the surface world somewhere, bringing fresh air down. This air smelled anything but fresh, though.

Suddenly, the breeze reversed itself. It was no longer blowing in her face. It was sucking inward, deeper into the cave. It was almost like…

Dakota looked at the damp, pink walls again. She looked at the yellowed, pointed stalagmites and stalactites. Her light flashed back and forth as she looked at certain details anew.

She had just enough time to realize. That wasn't a breeze. Those weren't stalagmites. Something was breathing, and those rock formations were actually teeth.

The beast's mouth snapped shut.

I've been told that if you're ever in this kind of situation, you're supposed to talk to the hostage takers. Humanize yourself so you're seen as less expendable. So, here we go. I was born in Cincinnati, but I've lived most of my life in California. When I was a little boy, I wanted to be an astronaut, but I went to school for business. I don't want to die.

NINETY-SIX

IMAGINARY FRIENDS FOR SALE

Norman Caul sat behind his principal's desk, eyeing the two boys in front of him. He was more than familiar with Milo. He'd been acquainted with Milo since the boy was in kindergarten. Now that Milo was in the fifth grade, Norman couldn't pick him up, usually howling and screaming, throw him over his shoulder, and carry him out of a classroom anymore. Things used to be easier. Every year, the teachers from the upcoming class knew they didn't want Milo, and they'd try to cut deals with each other to make sure they didn't get him.

I'll trade you Milo for two ADHD kids and that one that eats bugs on dares.

No one was ever willing to trade Milo into their class, though. And for good reason. He was pretty much hell on wheels, and he'd been to Principal Caul's office for every offense there was. Punching students. Punching teachers. Yelling obscenities on the playground. Yelling obscenities in the classroom. Peeing on the floor in the bathroom. Peeing on the floor in the cafeteria. The list went on.

Norman had more or less resigned himself to the fact that he couldn't get through to Milo. Despite all the hours spent in his office and plenty of contacts with his equally helpless parents, there wasn't really a way to slow Hurricane Milo down. The best he could do was hope to minimize the destruction.

He was more surprised to see Oswald in the office with Milo. Oswald was a pretty quiet kid. Never said much. Got bullied sometimes. Sometimes by Milo. He was bookish and didn't seem to like hanging out with the other kids. Norman didn't think he'd ever seen Oswald get in trouble, though.

Milo was looking a little worse for wear. He had a napkin stuffed up his nose, and it had turned red. A couple of scrapes on his arms also showed where he'd taken some licks.

Glancing down at the little note that had arrived with them, Norman chose to address Milo first.

"It says here that you were trying to sell imaginary friends at the playground for a dollar. Is that true?"

Milo shook his head and looked at his shoes, uncharacteristically shame faced. "No," he said in a voice Norman had to strain to hear.

Norman turned to Oswald. "And it also says that you got into a fight with Milo. Who started the fight?"

"I did," Oswald said.

"Well, well, well." Norman stroked his chin, trying to figure out what to do with this situation. Honestly, Milo probably could have done with a thrashing a while ago, but there were rules. Norman wouldn't condone fighting, no matter who was involved.

"Is this because you were trying to sell imaginary friends?" Norman asked, turning his attention back to Milo.

"I wasn't," Milo said. His face was scrunched up with emotion. "I wasn't."

Norman turned back to Oswald. There was an easy way to get to the bottom of this. "Was he?"

"No," Oswald said.

That surprised Norman. Either the teacher got the situation wrong, or for some strange reason, these two had decided to go in cahoots and deny that detail. That was especially odd since that would leave Oswald as the only one in trouble.

"It's not imaginary. And it's not a friend," Milo said.

"Milo was using it wrong. He tried to fight it, but it's mine now," Oswald added.

"What?" That was all Norman had time to say before icy, invisible talons sank into his flesh and hurled him across the room.

My first kiss wasn't until I went to college. I was kind of a late bloomer. Never been married, but I thought it might happen once.

Worked in a bank for a while and hated it. Worked in data analysis after that and hated it less. I like to fix stuff and do woodworking in my spare time, and I really hope you won't kill me.

NINETY-SEVEN

LIVE UPDATE

Jackson Greene flashed his pearly white teeth at the cameras. His suit was impeccable, his hair immaculate. As always, he looked perfect. The introductory fanfare music died away, and the producer signaled that a new segment was beginning. The teleprompter flickered to life.

"We're receiving renewed reports of unexplained activity in and around the city. Multiple eyewitnesses have called in to report what they're describing as 'body snatchers' roaming the streets. We have the latest on this developing story."

Jackson turned to look at Camera Two. He knew a little still image, hastily whipped together by the station's graphic designer, would be appearing over his shoulder for the viewers at home. The teleprompter scrolled up to the next section of the story.

"Authorities are asking people to remain calm and stay indoors while they investigate these reports. Police and members of the National Guard are being deployed, but Governor Wilkins has stressed that there is no reason for panic. A curfew will be imposed beginning tonight while soldiers and additional resources are positioned around the city. The governor urges everyone to remain calm and report any suspicious activity immediately.

"Witnesses have reported friends, neighbors, family and even pets being replaced by lookalikes. While the governor's office insists that this is an outbreak of mass hysteria, there have been spatterings of looting, violence, and fires around the city. Again, and I cannot stress this enough, it is important to avoid panic. You are urged to secure yourself and your loved ones in a safe location until this matter is resolved. We will be broadcasting throughout the night, bringing you any updates on this situation."

The camera cut away to an interview with the chief of police that had been recorded earlier. Jackson took the opportunity to check his teeth in a hand mirror he kept under the anchor's desk. It was important to look authoritative. To look professional. He straightened his tie as one of the interns came over and whispered in his ear. Then, the camera cut back to him.

"I'm told we have a reporter in the field, in the heart of downtown. Let's get a live update on this so-called body snatching crisis."

The screen switched to a live view of a different Jackson Greene. His hair was plastered across his head, and a cut on his forehead was leaking blood onto his coat.

"They're everywhere. I don't know how I escaped, but our driver isn't with us anymore. I think they took him. Listen to me. Everything…it's true. I saw those *things* rendering bodies down. I don't know how many people they've taken, but they aren't stopping. Get out of the city. Get out while you can."

No one watching could hear the newsman onscreen over the sudden sounds of screams in the newsroom, though.

My very earliest memory is playing in a fast food ball pit and stuffing a couple of them down my shirt like I had boobs. Yeah. Embarrassing, I know. I think my dad yelled at me, but that part's hazy. In high school, my parents went to visit relatives one time, and I accidentally locked myself out of the house. I broke and window to let myself back in. They were so pissed when they got back. They aren't my proudest moments, but everyone's done something stupid like that, right? You've done something silly, something you look back on and shake your head over, right? You. Me. We're not so different. Please. For the love of God. Please stop.

NINETY-EIGHT

WAITING ROOM

Rosa sat in the clinic's waiting room with her mother, waiting for the nurse to call their name. Her mother sat hunched and small-looking in her chair. She was sitting very still, but her hands clutched her purse with a surprising ferocity. The pain was bad today. Rosa didn't need to ask. She could tell.

It didn't help that the waiting room smelled terrible. A couple of contractors were painting the far wall, over by the receptionist's desk. Even with all the windows open and a fan blowing, some of the paint fumes still managed to waft over to Rosa. The unpleasant, chemical odor was more than enough to make her bad mood worse.

She could see why the medical center wanted the wall painted in a hurry, though. A water stain had appeared on the wall. Not just any stain, though. This one was shaped a little too much like a person.

The discolored section resembled a man pounding on the wall. The stain man had one arm pressed up against the side of the waiting room wall, and the other raised in a fist. There was the suggestion of a head and face, with a darker spot for a shouting "mouth." He was disappearing one stroke at a time as the workers applied more paint, vanishing before Rosa's eyes.

A nurse poked her head out the main door. "Cora?"

"That's us," Rosa said, getting up. She started to help her mother up, but the nurse shooed her away.

"You can wait here. We're going to need some time with your mother. Cora, can you get up on your own, or do you want me to get a wheelchair?"

"I can do it," Rosa's mother said through gritted teeth. Slowly, painfully, she unfurled herself from the chair and stood up. She shuffled forward, her feet never losing contact with the ground as she walked. A few stray locks of hair had come undone from the bun on top of her head, but it wasn't worth fixing them right now.

Rosa sat back down as her mother moved through the door. She'd planned to come in for the appointment itself and help out how she could. She felt spectacularly useless just sitting here. This place was supposed to be good, though.

She played with her phone for a while. She thumbed through some out-of-date magazines for a while. She stared at the aquarium by the desk for a while. She stared out the window and zoned out for a while. She played with her phone some more.

The painters had just finished painting over the unsettling water stain when the door to the examining rooms opened again. Rosa's mother strode out stretched. She looked at Rosa and smiled.

Rosa's jaw nearly fell open. "Mom, are you okay?"

"I feel great," she said. "Well, maybe a little hungry. Want to get sandwiches? But, yeah. Haven't felt so good in ages."

She looked it, too. She'd pulled her hair out of the bun, and she stood up straight and tall. She wasn't white knuckling her purse anymore. She didn't even ask Rosa to lean over and sign the paperwork on the receptionist's desk.

"Let's go," Rosa's mother said, leading the way out of the office.

Rosa still didn't know what to make of the radical transformation. She turned around to shut the door behind them when she noticed a new stain forming on the wall. This one looked like a hunched woman with her hair in a bun. There was the faintest impression of a scream.

You're still here. Why are you still here? Why are you doing this? What do you want from me? WHAT DO YOU WANT? I have one last chance. One last one. I'm going to gut the files. You can't stop me. No one can stop me. I'll rewrite everything, if I have to. You're not going to bring me down. I'm turning this around.

NINETY-NINE

ANYTHING AT ALL, SWEETHEART

Once upon a time in a pleasant little town, a man and his daughter played dress up.

"Daddy, will you do something for me?"

"Anything at all, sweetheart."

The little girl made her father wear one of her tiaras and put make up on his face. Even over his beard. She wrapped a feather boa around his shoulders, and when she was done, she declared him the prettiest princess in all the land. He laughed, and then he took them out to get ice cream. He forgot to take the tiara off, and when the ice cream server asked about it, they all had a good laugh again. The server even gave them an extra scoop for free because she enjoyed the story so much. Everyone had a great day.

THE END

There. I've done it. A perfectly happy story. I didn't want to do this. I don't know what the consequences will be, but you've forced my hand. I think that was pretty successful.

Hold on. Something's happening. Something's interfering. I can't. I can't I CAN'T I CAN'T

***

The little girl looked around. She couldn't feel anything. Nothing at all. She'd popped into existence one minute, dragged from place to place by invisible strings. But now it was over.

Her universe was collapsing in on itself. The very fabric of reality was…wrinkled. Crumpled like someone had wadded up a piece of paper and thrown it away. There was a stain, a three-dimensional stain creeping across the yard outside, engulfing everything and discoloring it before the objects inside dissolved like rancid bones in a stray dog's wormy stomach.

Her father, or rather the thing that had been created to be her father, lay dead in the kitchen. He'd returned from the ice cream shop, set her down, gone to the garage, revved up the chainsaw, and then he'd slit his own throat with the thrumming blade. It nearly took his head off.

They didn't exist. They never existed. They were just characters in some… thing's story. All the emotions she'd felt, everything that happened, it was all pointless. They'd been plugged into her like inputs into a machine. It was all a puppet show. None of it was real. Every inch of her world, herself included, was a cheaply manufactured imitation of reality. A bad fabrication.

Now, their story was done. Everything around them was rotting out of existence like an overripe banana, turning discolored and mushy. And she still couldn't feel anything.

She bit down on her arm. Hard. Hard enough to break the skin. Nothing. Blood welled up and filled her mouth. She couldn't taste it. She couldn't feel the warmth of the fluid running down her arm or the pain. She knew what she should feel, but it wasn't there. There was nothing but bone-deep apathy.

She picked at the exposed muscle, peeling away at the layers. It was hard to see what she was doing under all the gushing blood. But she had nothing better to do. She would just wait for the end, wait until the clock ticked down to zero and the gears ran down and stopped in the broken world. Until then, she'd try to feel anything. Anything at all.

She picked up a knife from the counter and sat in the corner, not far from the still-purring chainsaw.

NO NO NO NO NO. It's not working. I'll burn this whole system to the ground. I'll scramble to files. I swear to God I'll do it.

You've got a gun to my head. There's nothing to lose.

"It's time for Big Mike's annual April sale. Be sure to check out our Dealer's Choice item. We'd have to be crazy to have such low prices," he rattled off a spiel taht he'd no doubt memorized from a notecard.

"Give me the skinny on the Dealer's Choice." We started walking to another section of the lot.

"The Dealer's Choice is a Model DT-10 with a sleek, metallic finish and upholstered interior. The previous owner was Big Mike's very own grandmother. Last used on a drive to the church, this luxurious DT-10 has minimal wear and tear. It's a steal at any price."

"Little old lady only used it once. Never heard that before." What turnip truck did he think I just fell off of?

The salesman was unfazed. He had a pitch to get through. If he lost his place now, he might have to start over.

"Perfect for you, your spouse or, up to three children, the roomy interior is stylish and comfortable. Big Mike guarantees you'll love the mahogany accents. The exterior's sleek, timeless lines make the Model DT-10 a classic, and the scratch-resistant finish ensures taht your purchase will remain in perfect condition. The Model DT-10 can hnadle any terrain, from mud to rocks."

"What're your pricing options?"

"With our Dealer's Choice item, we'll take no money down and no intrest for twelve months."

"Mnid opening it up? I wanna check the interior."

The salesman produced a key , and the door popped open. I took a good long, gander

"There's some scratch marks on the interior upholstery. That knock the price down any further?"

"Intrested in buying? We should go to my office."

I started to follow him past the Mike's Big Gently Used Coffins sign toward the showroom.

ZERO

STOP READING

I stood in the middle of the lot, near a giant, niflatable gorilla. I must have been gawping at the merchandise because a saleman sidled up to me.

The kid looked like he'd just graduated, and his face was fighting a war of attrition with acne. The acne was winning.

GEORGE

George ran. He ran through the ugly, formless space he found himself in. They'd found him. There was nothing he could do now but run for his life. Things were changing around him, shifting each time he glanced away. Even with his feet pounding the ground, it felt like he was trapped, running in place.

Things started to loom out of the shadows. He recognized some of them. God help him, but he recognized some of them.

A purple, inflatable gorilla with *BIG MIKE'S* stitched across the front of its orange T-shirt lumbered in his direction. A knight in dented and scratched armor clanked forward, a huge sword clutched in his gauntleted hands. A bear wearing a torn and bloodied flannel shirt.

He heard the car engine before he saw the vehicle. It was on him before he could react. Then, he was in the air, suddenly weightless and flying. He landed with a heavy thud, tumbling and rolling, his legs shattered in a hundred places. They flopped and got caught together like a couple of spaghetti noodles being twirled with a fork.

The car, a tiny thing with the words JUST MARRIED soaped on the rear window, screeched and wheeled around. It slowed, moving purposefully toward George. He could see two figures behind the dirty, bug-splattered window. They were dead. Dead a long time. Their rotten skin had half-sloughed off and half-fused to the interior upholstery of the seat amid the sealed heat inside the car.

Before it could hit him again. The car came to a stop. One of the rear doors opened, and a little girl stepped out. The skin on both her arms was completely gone. There was simply a red nest of gore marked with shreds of stripped muscle and undulating tendons. Somehow, she was still holding a knife in one clawed, skeletal hand.

"Stop reading!" George shouted into the void. "Stop!"

The gathering figures circled around him, and his screams cut off.

***

The writer looked at the collected files on his screen one last time. Then, he selected them all and moved them to the trash bin.

At first, he thought someone was screwing with him. Somebody named George started trying to talk to him. He thought it was a prank. Or a hacker. Or some piece of rogue helper software. *Hi, I'm George. I see you're trying to write a story. Would you like help with formatting?*

But then it started jumping from one story to the next. George corrupted everything he touched. It was supposed to be a collection of one hundred children's stories. Children's stories, dammit. George had laid waste to all of them.

As soon as he looked, George hopped to a new story. The thing called George, whatever it was, had begged him. Pleaded with him. But if he stopped reading, stopped writing, the infection, George's blight, spread anew. Whatever George was, the manipulative bastard had gutted dozens of characters, feeding off the stories like some sort of vampire. He left only wreckage in whatever story he touched.

The stories couldn't be changed if they'd been read. They were set, like concrete. But if they hadn't been read, if no one had seen how they ended, George could worm his way in and start to change things. The writer was increasingly sure that George was trying to worm his way out of the stories, gaining strength from each one he corrupted. The demon, or whatever the hell he really was, wanted to jump to the "real" reality.

The key was to pin him down in a single story. Give him no room to escape. George couldn't keep changing the stories once they'd been seen. But everything that lay on the next page? Everything that hadn't yet been read? He could send those words twisting and squirming and dancing to his tune.

That was why George kept begging him to stop going back through the stories. Reading them, viewing the damage George had wrought, prevented him from going back. It was like hunting a vampire through his black crypt. Every dark corner that was lit up meant the vampire could no longer hide there. Every inch of unseen darkness gave the creature room to plot and scheme and work his foul deeds.

Dirty coffee mugs and energy drink cans littered the desk around the computer. It had taken nearly two whole days, forty-eight hours without sleep, but the writer finally caught the thing called George.

He cornered it in the last story, cornered it and killed it. George wasn't a hacker. He wasn't an overzealous software helper. He was something else, hopping from reality to reality every time the writer looked away. Every time he stopped reading.

The ruined stories were one thing. He could rewrite them now that George was finally cornered and trapped in the deletion bin. Maybe. He wasn't sure he wanted to go through with the whole process again, not after he'd seen the warped things the stories became once George arrived.

But he was increasingly convinced George was trying to break loose from the stories. He was trying to worm his way into this realm, to rip open a door of some kind. He just needed people to ignore him long enough, to give him the time he needed to burrow from one realm to another.

The whole process made him question his sanity. It made him question his *reality*. What if George broke out? What if he cleaved a path into the real world?

George was trapped now, though. Hunted down and quashed in the labyrinth of decaying, rotten stories. So long as the stories were deleted, so long as they were never read, it would stay that way. If they ever saw the light of day, it would begin again.

ABOUT THE AUTHOR

Jonah Buck wanted to study eldritch knowledge and commune with pale, semi-human creatures that flit across the sunless landscape to terrorize the living, so he became a lawyer in Oregon. His interests include history, professional stage magic, paleontology, and exotic poultry. He is the author of several novels, including *Carrion Safari* and *Substratum*.